THE ISLAND

THE MADION WAR TRILOGY

S. Usher Evans

D0162514

Sun's Golden Ray Publishing

THE MADION WAR TRILOGY

The Island
The Chasm
The Union

Line Editing by Danielle Fine
Madion War Trilogy logo designed by Anita@Race-Point.com
Phoenix and Lion Icons courtesy of VectorPortal.com
Copyright © 2016 Sun's Golden Ray Publishing

ISBN: 0986298174
ISBN-13: 978-0986298172

CONTENTS

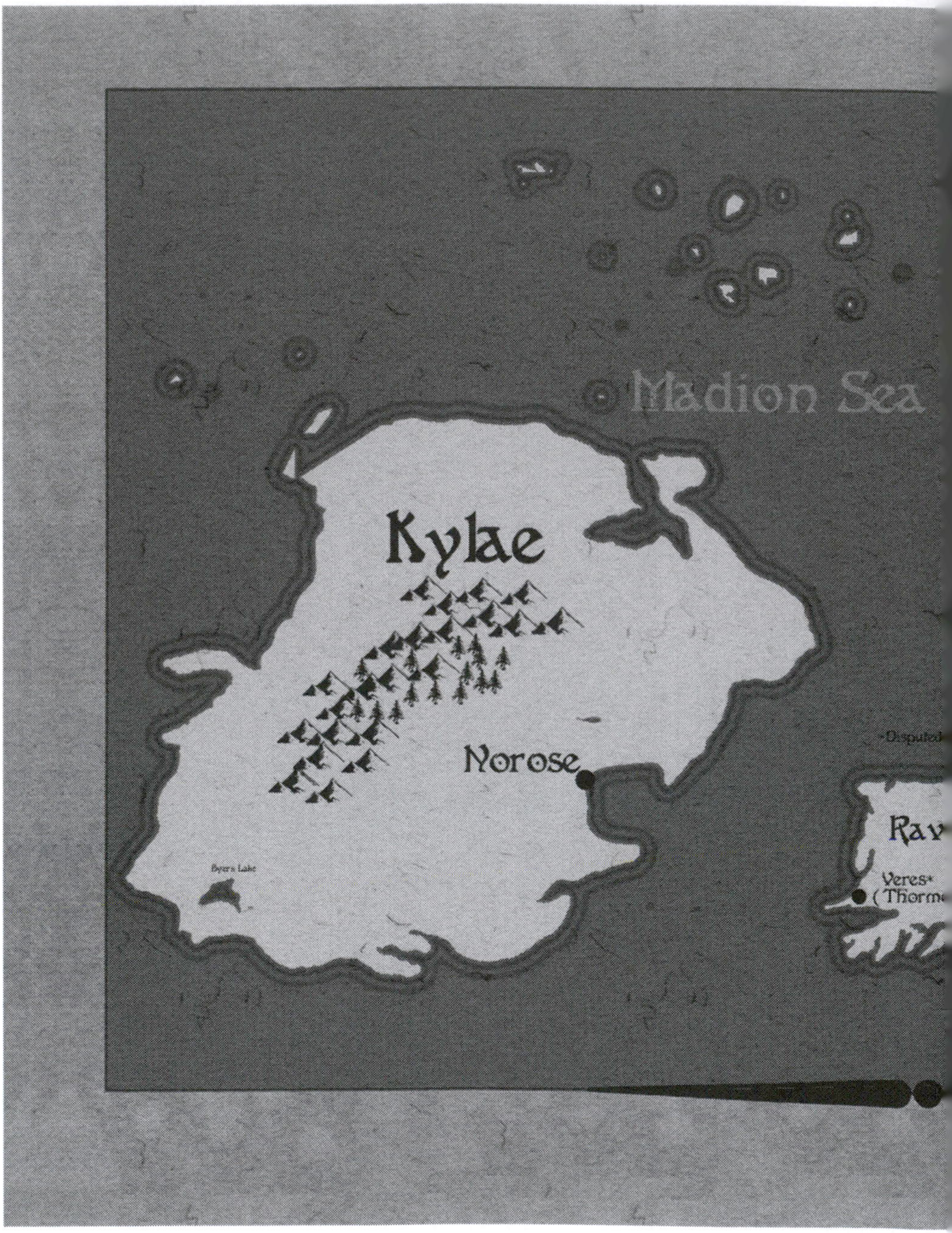
Madion Sea
Kylae
Norose
Veres

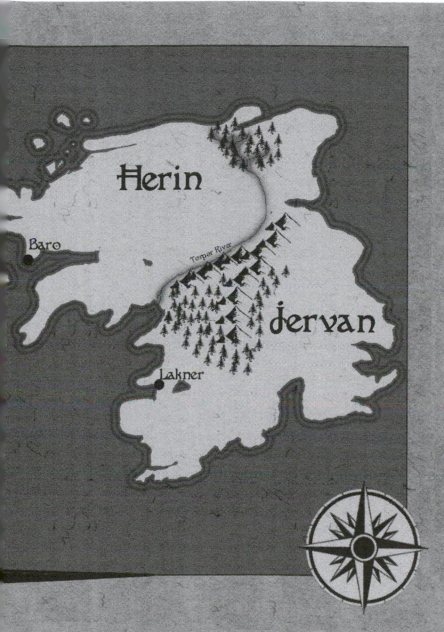

Fifty years ago,

Citing the gross abuse of its people and resources, the Raven people declared their independence from the kingdom of Kylae.

The Madion War has raged on ever since.

ONE

THEO

"Oi, *Kallistrate.*"

Zlatan could have been referring to any one of ten of the air force pilots in the crowded locker room. *Kallistrate* was the Raven word for orphan and in this war-torn country, there were more of us without parents than with. But the disrespectful tone was proof enough that Zlatan was talking to me. After all, I was the only female in the vicinity who outranked him.

My lieutenants watched us, a sea of dark faces and white eyes wide in nervous excitement. Zlatan was a brute, thickset and entitled, an older addition to our ranks who liked to throw his weight around to the younger pilots. He'd never directly tussled with me before, and I was interested to see how far he would go.

"I heard you bragging to Lanis about that skirmish last week," Zlatan sneered at me with his round face and eyes crowded a little too close together.

"You mean my debrief?" I said casually. "As a *captain*, part of my duties are to report the outcome of a mission to leadership."

The emphasis of my rank did not go unnoticed. The other pilots snickered as his already dark face grew more so.

"You think you're pretty good, huh? Surviving a couple dogfights don't make you no better than the rest of us," he snarled.

I'd never had much of an ego, especially when it came to idiots, so I turned to my locker and began stripping out of my jumpsuit.

Zlatan had a different idea. He grabbed my shoulder and spun me around, his putrid breath in my space. "Captain or not, you don't turn your back on me, *bitch*."

In response, I kneed him hard in the groin, and he fell to his knees, his face red with pain. The other pilots let out a cheer—every one of them was hoping Zlatan wouldn't return one day. But he had a nasty habit of faking illness whenever the sirens wailed and called us to defend our country.

As Zlatan howled and cried, I finished changing out of my jumpsuit and left the crowded locker room before I attracted any more trouble.

I wasn't in the mood to celebrate a fellow Raven's beating, even one who so tantalizingly deserved it. My captain's training course had made it clear that I was to be a leader, to keep morale high. Ever since declaring our independence from the nation of Kylae some fifty years ago, we'd been under constant attack as the bastards kept trying to bring us back into the fold. The forward operating base at Vinolas was the first line of defense against Kylae's aerial attacks on the northern coast of our island nation, but we were woefully understaffed and undertrained. I had a squadron of twenty pilots, most of whom were teenagers, conscripted at the age of twelve and barely trained before showing up to fly for me.

However, only nineteen had returned from this morning's

mission, I noted with a grimace. I tried not to think about who I hadn't seen in the locker room.

After the morning's surveillance and the skirmish with Zlatan, I was eager to find quiet. I hadn't really known any other home but metal bunkbeds and gruel, so the large dormitory was welcoming to me. I'd long ago learned how to create a privacy bubble for myself, even in the presence of two hundred other pilots jammed in there.

But before I could climb into bed, there was commotion at the end of the giant hall where we slept. A group of still-uniformed young girls huddled around a bed, crying and wailing. I didn't know them, but I knew the sound. They'd known the pilot who hadn't returned. Although we hadn't encountered any enemies, our equipment was old and failed regularly when not maintained. Those who didn't learn how to change oil or check for problems didn't make it very long.

My sanctuary was calling, but my humanity was louder. With a deep breath, I approached the miserable circle and forced a grim smile onto my face. When they noticed me, one of them had the state of mind to stand, but I waved her off with a small shake of my head.

"What was her name?" I should've been used to these conversations, but I couldn't keep the crack of emotion out of my voice.

"Marij." The girls couldn't have been older than thirteen or fourteen, and this seemed to be their first loss of a friend. I wished I could tell them it would be their last.

I struggled to push out the words that I'd been trained to say since I'd been promoted. "Marij died in the cause of Raven independence. There is no greater honor."

The sentiment fell flat on the girls, but one of them half-smiled at me. "Thank you, 'neechai."

I bristled at the Raven word for "sister"—it wasn't so much a translation, but a sentiment. The old Raven language had long since faded away into the common tongue, but we'd retained some words that just didn't translate. *Oneechai* meant more than just a blood sister; it was a familiar woman who tended to others, who felt like a warm embrace. Someone who was always there. It wasn't a term Ravens threw around lightly.

Although I never corrected them, I hated it when my subordinates used it to describe me. I could never protect them as well as an *oneechai* should, not when I lost two or three of my pilots every week. And yet, every week, more kids showed up, looking to me to save them from almost certain death as they got into their planes and headed off to battle.

And to save my own heart, I'd stopped learning their stories, stopped learning their names—I even stopped looking at their faces. It didn't matter though; the pain was the same.

With a grim smile and a pat on the shoulder, I turned to leave the girls, and I couldn't help but wonder which one would be mourned next.

GALIAN

"We will send the second wave in the Birgdorn formation, attacking their right flank. The first wave will then target the armory at Vinolas F.O.B."

I blinked as my father's general droned on about his great

military strategy. I was sure it was well thought-out and considered, but I just didn't care. My uniform was itchy and uncomfortable, and the monotone voice was putting me to sleep. But I resisted the strong urge to sigh, as my father's beady eyes were trained on me. Especially now, based on how he'd opened this meeting of his most senior military leadership.

"You will take part in this battle, son," he'd said.

My father rarely called me son in front of his generals. My mother said it was to avoid calling attention to our relationship, but I doubted there was a person alive in Kylae who didn't know my face. I was the third son of King Grieg and Queen Korina. My older brother, Rhys, was well on his way to taking the throne whenever His Highness died (because retirement was not an option), and my second older brother, Digory, had already given his life in service to our country.

Which was why I was now sitting in this room full of generals, being instructed on how to execute a surprise attack on Rave.

We always called it a "surprise," but I doubted that Rave would have been able to do much even if we sent them a courtesy message of, "Hey, we're coming to bomb you tomorrow."

Rave was our colony, the site of a fifty-year rebellion that we were still fighting to quash. They'd built a sham government during that time, elected a few dozen corrupt officials and conscripted millions of their citizens to fight in the senseless war. I personally thought my father should've just let them go off and be their own country, as his rule wasn't much better, but I didn't dare voice that opinion. The Kylaen war machine was our biggest industry, putting hundreds of thousands of our citizens to work every year, and the backbone of our thriving economy.

My place, up until last year, had been in our prestigious

hospital. I'd just begun my residency after spending four grueling years as a medical student. I'd been in the middle of assisting in my first surgery when I learned that my older brother, Digory, had been shot down in the ocean.

We'd had a huge funeral procession for him, flags at half-staff for weeks, big speeches about the importance of our cause and Kylaen pride and blah, blah, blah. It wasn't two days after we'd gotten the news, that my father began to not-so-subtly hint that it was time for me to trade in my stethoscope for a pilot's helmet. Which was how I'd ended up a captain or something ridiculously unearned, in my father's military. I'd finally mastered the art of getting the plane in the air, and getting it back on the ground, and now they were sending me into battle.

I probably should've been paying attention to what the general was saying as little Kylaen planes buzzed across the screen, showing different attack formations, but I just couldn't. Ever since I had started flying, every single instructor had said the same thing:

Act normal.

Stay out of trouble.

Fly away if they find out it's you.

I wondered if they'd said the same thing to Digory, but knowing my late brother, he'd probably told them to go to hell. Which was how he'd ended up a floating corpse in the Madion Sea. Idiot.

It may sound like I didn't grieve my brother. I did, but he'd been a real asshole and I didn't miss the way he'd terrorized me.

My ears perked up when chairs scraped on the ground, and people rose to their feet. Elijah Kader, the head of my personal bodyguard contingent, was already tapping his foot impatiently when I walked out of the conference room.

"Sire, are you ready to leave?" He even managed to say it without the usual acidic tone. Ever since he'd shown up to drive me one day instead of my usual palace guards, he had made it clear that protecting the spare prince was somewhat of a demotion for him.

"Yeah, I'm ready." Dread swam in the bottom of my stomach at the thought of bombing and killing innocent civilians—even if they were Ravens.

"Sarge, there's a group of 'em waiting outside already." Dave Martin was a two-striper a couple years younger than me. He was one of the only guys who didn't seem to hate being assigned to watch over a prince.

"Did you tell anyone you were coming here?" Kader growled at me.

I glared at him. "Because I love being hounded by those assholes. No."

Kader muttered colorful curses under his breath and cracked open the door to the hangar where my official car was parked. There was a crowd of people, most of whom had cameras hanging around their necks.

The Kylaen tabloids. Perfect.

Since nobody in Kylae was interested in a fifty-year war anymore, the media delighted in telling stories about the royal family. I had almost outgrown my reputation as a carefree party boy by the time I'd finished medical school, but now my new title was "Dashing Pilot," and the media were back in their incessant stalking of me. There was a media blackout on my actual missions—for my safety, of course—but they loved catching a photo of me in uniform. At least it was better than the stories about my partying and womanizing, which were woefully overblown.

I steeled myself and put on the most stoic face I could muster as I nodded to Kader. The moment the door opened, the flashes began, as did the questions.

"Prince Galian!"

"Sire, over here!"

"Sire, is it true you're dating Olivia Collins?"

I sniffed at that last one; I had no idea who that girl was, and I sure as hell wasn't dating her. But the tabloids did love to concoct stories when I didn't have any to tell.

Kader pushed a photographer aside to open my door and I slid in, thankful for the tinted windows and the privacy of my car.

"To the castle?" Kader asked, sounding as if he would have rather told me to go somewhere else.

"Actually," I said, looking at the hangar again where, in a few short hours, I would be taking off to bring death and destruction to Rave, "let's pop by the hospital."

Kader made a noise, but his military training wouldn't let him disagree with me. He put the car in drive and we left the crowd of photographers behind, although I was sure some of them would follow us. They always did.

THEO

Walking into the hangar was like coming home. I'd grown up there, so I knew every nook and cranny of the cavernous room. I paused at a wall adorned with photos and newspaper clippings and pressed two fingers to the Raven symbol in the center in a superstitious show of reverence. It resembled a phoenix (since we considered ourselves reborn from our former colony), with long tail feathers and giant claws that reached out for our future, so they said. I always thought it a pretty decent depiction of the Raven spirit—small, scrappy, and determined.

Around the Raven symbol, we'd plastered photos of the Kylaen royal family cut out from magazines and newspapers to remind us of who we were fighting against. There was King Greig, balding with black, coifed facial hair. Next to him was his wife Korina, the daughter of one of Kylae's wealthiest families. A beautiful woman with the prized porcelain skin so desired by Kylaen designers. She was nothing but a pushover; a woman who'd stood in front of the Kylaen death camp and swore it wasn't as bad as it was.

They had three sons, Rhys, Digory, and Galian, whose pictures were lined up next. I took pleasure in seeing the center boy, Digory, a bulky brute of a man who had been killed in action last year. We'd celebrated for three days when the news came over the radio that Kylae had lost one of her precious princes. Rhys was the next in line to be king, and seemed to be of the same mold as his father and grandfather. We saw him standing behind his father at news conferences and ceremonies, saying nothing as his father continued the tirade against Rave.

And then there was the princeling.

We had several photos of the third son of Kylae, most of which were cut from Kylaen gossip magazines. Tall, broad-shouldered, with that Kylaen pale skin and smoldering dark eyes, he was every bit the playboy prince. In one photo, he was on the arm of two different girls, and in another, he was vomiting in the streets. For a few years, it seemed a new story would break about his antics almost every week, embarrassing his father and a kingdom in the midst of a bloody war. But we had seen less and less of him—probably thanks to the Kylaen royal family.

Then suddenly, we'd found out he was taking his brother's place in the Kylaen air forces. Now it was only a matter of time before one of us shot him down and claimed our prize. Personally, I hoped it would be me. Perhaps killing the princeling would accelerate my own promotion and hasten my escape from danger.

The hangar was empty of pilots and activity after the morning's patrol, but the mechanics were hard at work, trying to service as many planes as possible. If the Raven military was light on pilots, they were absolutely abysmal on ground crew.

My twin-propeller plane was right where I had left her when I rolled in from my morning air patrol. She was the only friend I had in this whole world, and it was a mutually beneficial relationship. If she didn't fail me, and I didn't fail her, we'd both survive. Six years after my first flight, we were both still kicking. I knew my girl inside and out, knew just how far I could push her before she began to smoke up, knew how to land her and take her off like the back of my hand. Sliding into the cockpit was probably what it was like to be with a man, but since I'd never done that, I could only guess. In any case, it was warm and familiar.

"Hey, Theo!" Lanis called to me from the plane next to mine. He was covered in oil from the plane he was working on. "Good patrol this morning?"

"Yeah," I said, checking the oil levels on my ship and continuing my routine inspection. "What do you hear on the next mission?"

"Eh," he grunted. "Bayard was on the radio this morning, talking about how we're winning the fight against Kylaen aggression. That Cannon guy is still with him."

I snorted; our president had been reelected four times in the past fifteen years, and the president before that had been in power since we first declared independence from Kylae. Bayard was the consummate politician, and had been known to keep war heroes by his side at press conferences. His latest pet project was Mark Cannon, a handsome captain who'd fought off twenty planes on the western front.

"So what do you hear about the mission?" I pressed. The old man had been around; he'd been a pilot himself in his younger days, retiring after his twenty years in the service and coming back as a mechanic. But he retained his connections to the other pilots who'd gone on to become the higher ranking bigwigs in our military. So he always knew the secrets.

"The princeling is about ready to start flying," he said, looking around. At my startled gasp, he added, "Now don't be spreading that around, 'neechai.'"

"I won't, I won't," I shook my head and smiled. Coming from someone like Lanis, the Raven pet name meant more like little sister. Raven words were funny like that.

But the princeling out in the air? That was good news. "Grieg is really sending his son out even after the other one was killed last year?"

"Yep." Lanis nodded. "Turns out they made an upstanding citizen out of that playboy." He winked at me. "Don't go losing your head over him like these other girls."

"Me? Please!" But I had to laugh. Galian was not wanting for handsomeness, and he'd managed to steal the hearts of more than one of my fellow female pilots. Somehow they could separate him from his family and his country, something I'd never been able to do.

"You'd better keep an eye on some of your lieutenants." Lanis laughed. "They find out the princeling is up in the sky with you, they'll follow him back to the castle—hoping they can become a princess!"

"Well, then they can follow him down to hell, 'cause if I see him up there, that's where he's going," I said, holding my fingers up to the sky and making a shooting sound. "Down he goes like his brother."

"Just look for the one who can't fly, right?" Lanis laughed and I joined him, the absurdity of the situation so very amusing.

"I'm not looking for anything if my plane doesn't get off the ground," I said, grabbing a wrench. I needed to work quickly. I never knew when the air raid sirens would begin to wail.

GALIAN

The Kylaen hospital was world-renowned for the quality of care provided. Doctors from all nations flocked here to take advantage of the research and most technologically advanced tools, and only the best doctoral candidates were accepted as interns and residents. Except if you were the son of the man paying all the bills. Then you just got in.

The medical staff was led by the chief of medicine, Dr. Sebastian Maitland. He'd been my own doctor since I was in diapers, and one of the reasons I'd decided to go into medicine. Even before I put on my first lab coat, he was always available to dispense wisdom and guidance, and he was the man I wanted to see before this stupid farce of an air raid.

He met me at the entrance to the hospital, undoubtedly tipped off to my arrival by trailing tabloid photographers. As soon as I fought my way past them, I shook the hand of my mentor. His bald head was covered in age spots, but he was as spry and as agile as ever.

"Your Highness!" I had begged him to lose the formalities a long time ago, but it was rare that he called me by my given name. "How goes the flying?"

"Ugh. I've got...a thing in a few hours." Even though I trusted Maitland with my life, Raven had become desperate lately with their spying. I wouldn't put it past them to have a spy stationed at the hospital.

"In the meantime, we are understaffed today," he said with a knowing sparkle in his eye. "Perhaps I could persuade you to step in and help examine some of them?"

He didn't have to ask twice. As quickly as I could retrieve them from my locker (which they'd kept out of respect for me), I was back in my lab coat and scrubs, following Dr. Maitland as he did his morning rounds. We paused at the nurse's station to get the latest, and I ignored the gaga-eyes from a young blonde while the head nurse spoke to Dr. Maitland. She recommended we pay a visit to a veteran in room four, as he was there alone without any family. I was pretty sure she only suggested it on my account, but I was more than willing to play "Prince Doctor" for one of our veterans. Or at least, that was what I'd tell my father later today when he asked why I returned to the hospital instead of prepping for the mission that afternoon.

"It's...His Highness!"

The man was seventy, in the hospital with a broken hip from

slipping down some stairs. He began trying to get out of bed to bow to me, but I stepped forward quickly to keep him from reinjuring himself.

"Please," I said, gently pushing him back to bed. "Please sit back down."

"Bless you, sire," he whispered. He gripped my hands with his old, weathered ones, and smiled. Dr. Maitland quizzed me on the patient's chart and my recommended procedure, and it helped ease some of my worry. Being in that room, talking medicine instead of war, felt right.

A nurse popped her head in to request Dr. Maitland's assistance with another patient, so he left me in the room to continue by myself. I glanced through the chart three times before I actually read anything. I questioned the patient on his pain levels and then, remembering what the nurse had said, asked him about his family.

"Never had one," he said. "Spent twenty years in the Kylaen forces before I retired."

The reminder that I was getting ready to go into battle and kill a bunch of people was unwelcome, and I let the grimace show on my face.

"Sire? Did I say something to offend you?"

"No," I said. "I'm just... Can you keep a secret?"

"Of course." He nodded.

"I'm sure you know I...joined the Kylaen forces," I said, hoping I didn't sound too bitter. "Today is my very first air raid. And to be perfectly frank, I don't think...well, it doesn't sit right with me."

"Sire, I, too, was a pilot in our great Kylaen forces, on behalf of your grandfather. The Ravens are better off under Kylaen rule, and it's only their misguided need to be independent that causes their suffering. They're squandering freedom as it is."

I smiled and thanked the man, squeezing his hand and asking if there was anything else I could get for him then left. His words would've had more impact if I hadn't seen them blazed across propaganda posters, or spoken at my brother's funeral to try to appease my grieving mother's heart.

Dr. Maitland met me outside with a grim smile on his face. "Your sergeant is waiting for you at the nurse's station," he said quietly. "He said you're needed back at the airfield."

My heart fell into my stomach. Dr. Maitland, perceptive as ever, offered to walk me to his office to delay the inevitable a bit longer.

"I hate this," I said, finally, as he closed the door behind him. "My stupid father—"

Dr. Maitland cut me off. "Sire, your father simply is trying to stem the tide of the war."

"Yeah, I'd believe that if he'd quit starting all the fights," I noted, watching the old doctor bristle. Dr. Maitland and I had spoken at length about my father since I was old enough to have a problem with him, but the good doctor was never comfortable when I disparaged His Highness.

"I have a gift for you," Dr. Maitland said, retrieving a black bag from under his desk and handing it to me. "For your first mission."

The bag was filled with medical supplies—antibacterial wipes, needles and tubes, gloves. I looked up at him dubiously. "I doubt I'm ever going to need these in the air."

"Galian, you're a perceptive sort of fellow, one who I've had the utmost pleasure watching grow from an inquisitive boy into a very well-rounded and genuinely kind young man. I was so proud when you asked me to help you apply for medical school, and even prouder when you joined me here at the hospital."

"Will you be proud of me when I kill someone today?" I asked before I could stop myself.

"I believe you will do what is necessary for your safety and the safety of those around you," Dr. Maitland said. "Including any Ravens."

I glanced up at him, confused.

"Galian, you know we get all kinds of patients in this hospital," he began quietly, and I knew this conversation was to stay between us. "I don't have the luxury of discriminating between Kylaen and Raven patients when they come into my hospital bleeding to death. I heal who needs to be healed, and leave politics to your father.

"I'm giving you this bag not to use, but to remind you that you are not..." He paused, swallowing. "You are not your father's man. You are your own, and you can choose to do whatever you will with the time given to you."

I was shocked at the boldness of his words, and knew he was breaking his own strict code to say them. But I also needed to hear them.

He smiled at me with sadness in his eyes. "Good luck, Your Highness."

TWO

THEO

BEEP. BEEP. BEEP.

I looked up from my engine, my heart sinking into my stomach. Our radar had picked up an incoming Kylaen attack. No matter how many times I'd heard the alarm, it never got any less frightening.

But I had no time for fear, not when my twenty (*nineteen*, I reminded myself) pilots needed me to lead the way.

I quickly finished the work on my engine, touching each of the screws to ensure I had fastened them. Lanis had taught me that trick—one loose screw could be the difference between life and death.

My pilots trickled into the hangar and crowded around me as they had been instructed. I forced myself to speak some words of support.

"They've been targeting the armory the last few attacks," I said, my voice strong and authoritative. "Don't let them get past you. We haven't yet rebuilt the facility after last year. Don't let them set us back again."

I could've gone on about the importance of Raven independence or any of the other topics I'd memorized, but it wouldn't have done much good. Most of my pilots wore their nervousness on their faces, their fear that these moments in this place were their last. And I knew that, for some, it was.

Instead of a speech, I smiled grimly. "Good luck. Dismissed."

The group of twenty (*nineteen*) dispersed to their ships and, after a moment, I turned and walked to my girl. Once more, I touched the bolts on the engine, making sure the torque marks I'd placed were still intact, as were the older marks. Confident my girl was ready for battle, I closed up the hatch and said a small prayer.

"*'neechai*," Lanis called. I followed his gaze to one of my ships still in the hangar, the pilot unmoving inside. I hurried to him, avoiding the other planes as they taxied out of the hangar. When I reached his plane, I climbed up to sit on top of the nose. The young pilot didn't even acknowledge my presence.

"Hey...Dobolek, right?" I said, reading the name on his uniform. He nodded slightly. "First mission?"

"Yes *'neechai*."

"It's not so bad," I said, hoping I sounded convincing. Nothing really compared to the sickening fear that came with one's first flight. But I needed him to get out there and try to survive.

"My brothers are dead. My friends died in training. Why should I get in this plane and go to my own death?"

I hated this question. I hated it because I had no good answers for it. It was one thing to talk about honor and country and duty, but when faced with a thirteen-year-old who was asking why he had to die, I could never force out the words I'd been told to say.

Instead, I told him the same thing I said to myself every time I got in a plane:

"Look, you survived training. You survived a Raven childhood. You've come all the way to this point. And God wouldn't have let you survive this long if there wasn't a reason."

He nodded as two tears ran down his face.

"So maybe you die today, or maybe you make it back with the rest of us. But whatever happens—"

"Theo!" Lanis called. "Radar tower's wondering where you are!"

I waved to Lanis, and he understood.

"Take all that fear and trust that someone else is in control. There's nothing else that you can do," I said, taking his hand and squeezing it. "I'll be right up there with you."

I hopped off his plane and stood back, waiting and hoping that my speech had at least jarred him enough to get him to move. And yet, I didn't want him to go. I wanted him and the rest of my twenty (*nineteen*) pilots back in their bunks where they belonged.

But at the same time, if we didn't go out there, the Kylaens would drop their bombs on our base, killing us anyway.

With that thought firmly lodged in my own mind, I marched back to my plane, ready to defend my country.

Galian

Butterflies filled my stomach. I hadn't quite relaxed since I left the hospital, and now, as I flew over the beautiful blue Madion Sea, my hands shook on the joystick of my plane.

I couldn't have told anyone what we were trying to accomplish. I could barely even remember my name.

There hadn't been anyone to see me off, though Kader had gripped me hard on my shoulder before I'd walked into the hangar. I checked all my instruments again, although our ships were so heavily modified, they basically flew themselves these days. In the distance, the first wave of pilots was engaging with the Raven forces. I was part of the third wave, the backup to the backup. Some part of me wished that a miracle would happen before my part in this exercise began, and we'd all turn around and go back home.

In my helmet, I heard the sounds of the pilots ahead of me, their cursing and hissing as they avoided being blown up.

"Aargh!"

I swallowed hard as a plume of fire exploded around one of the planes in the distance. Scratchy voices came through from our airfield some two hundred miles behind me, ordering in the second wave of forces.

But the Ravens had gone on the offensive, nearly twenty planes headed straight for the third wave. Bullets flew and I turned my ship to the side to avoid being shot. A Raven plane zoomed too close for comfort. Unlike our advanced planes with a single propeller, they still had the twin props on their rusty, older models.

"First wave, disengage from mission and provide cover," someone barked in my ear.

A bright flame exploded to my right and there was screaming in my ear again as another Kylaen soldier went down. Martin's young face was in my mind's eye, and I imagined he was in the plane that just went down, even though he was waiting with Kader back in Norose. Perhaps

I could stomach it if I thought of this as an exercise in protecting my fellow soldiers versus killing innocent people.

I flew my ship high above the rest, firing half-hearted bullets toward the rickety old ships that, despite looking older than I was, were still holding their own against our modern planes. I'd even begun to root for the Ravens; if they fought us off too badly, we'd retreat back to Norose.

A familiar voice floated through our secure channels.

"Well, boys, looks like you're kicking some ass out there..."

It was Rhys, my eldest brother and the heir to the throne. He was technically in the military as well, but only dropped in on special occasions. My first mission apparently counted.

Truthfully, his voice calmed my nerves. It was nice to know he was back at the airfield supporting me.

I switched on my microphone and hoped I sounded brave.

"Hey asshole. They let you in the front door?"

Something changed in the radio chatter, and a chorus of voices began talking quickly and frantically. My radio went out for a second and I fiddled with the controls—

A bullet flew by my head, and I stared at the exit hole on my cockpit glass. If it had been an inch closer, I might have been looking at my splattered brains on the window.

As if my mind were working in slow motion, I realized that I must've alerted our enemy that I was among them. Of course they'd been monitoring our channels and recognized my voice.

And now, they were gunning for me.

"Galian, get out of there!" Rhys's voice was in my ear, rising above the fracas and giving me permission to do the thing I'd been wanting to do all day.

THEO

I had the princeling.

By my count, we'd lost fifteen planes of the two hundred in our base's fleet. I didn't know how many of mine were included in that number. It was an oddly populated battle, with more Kylaen airships than usual coming at us in their normal wave formation.

I'd shot down four planes when a stagnant plane flying high overhead caught my attention. There was something about the way he flew. Careful, not engaging in the fight. Then word came over the speakers that they'd heard the princeling over the radio, talking to his brother back in Kylae. I just *knew* that if I shot that plane out of the sky, we'd soon hear word that the Raven military had claimed another Kylaen royal.

Call it a gut feeling.

When the plane turned and headed north, I left the melee in the air behind, knowing if I took my eyes off of it for a second, he could disappear.

I'd be damned if I'd let him go.

Several Kylaen airships followed me, but I hadn't survived five years of this shit for nothing. I rolled my ship, took a few sharp turns, all the normal evasive maneuvers to lose them. And when that didn't work, I cracked open the small emergency window on my cockpit and stuck my gun out, firing at their fuselages. Two explosions later, they were falling into the Madion sea below us.

"*Whoop!* Captain Kallistrate, you have points for style!"

I grinned as one of my fellow pilots came flying up beside me, taking out the other plane.

The princeling had gained some distance while I was losing his contingent of bodyguards, and I put on a burst of speed to follow him.

"Stand down. This one's mine."

GALIAN

After a while, with no sign of anyone tailing me, I slowed my plane and put my hand over my racing heart. Though I'd seen death before, I had never been so close to my own. I don't know why my brother was so eager to get out there.

I glanced behind me and saw I'd put a healthy distance between me and the battle. I had done as instructed, and when it seemed like they were targeting me, I had escaped. Like a weakling.

An alive weakling, my inner voice answered.

I reminded myself that I was royal, that I had a duty in case anything happened to Rhys.

But he was safe in Norose. So I really was a big chicken for flying away.

I was following orders.

Chicken.

"Damn it." I sighed, speaking aloud to quiet the internal

bickering. There was nothing but static in my helmet now, a sign that I was too far away from the towers at Norose to hear what was going on.

"Hello? Anybody there?" I asked.

When no one responded, I slumped in my seat and banged my head against the headrest. I was still gliding over the blue ocean, heading north. I turned my ship to the west to head back to Norose—or at least get within range of the tower to get further directions.

What was my father going to say when he found out I'd turned tail and run? What would the soldiers think? Would they even be able to look at me?

"Rhys? Anybody?" I asked into the static.

Maybe Father wouldn't be too pissed at me; Rhys *had* told me to leave. I could always blame him. Rhys wasn't infallible, but he seemed to get away with a lot more than I ever could.

I sniffed at the irony. I was more afraid of my father than being blown out of the sky.

At least, I was until I saw a glint of metal in the distance.

"Hey, who's there?" I asked, my voice less shaky than before. Static answered me again.

I squinted at the ship I was about to encounter and my blood ran cold.

They'd found me.

THEO

I was Captain Theo Kallistrate, and I was going to kill a Kylaen royal.

He was coasting along a northwesterly path—no doubt trying to sneak back into Kylae without having to engage. What a coward, leaving behind his own troops. But I expected nothing more from that bloodline.

I smelled burning oil, but my engine temperature was still within normal range, so I figured I might have a leak. Nothing to be concerned about. I trusted my plane to keep me safe.

I aimed my guns and fired, bullets spraying from the nose toward the Kylaen ship. The princeling maneuvered out of the way and fired back, but his aim was atrocious. It was good to see him attempting to show some backbone. It would make killing him that much more satisfying.

He bolted north again, but I wasn't going to let him get away. Kylaen ships were fast, but so was my girl. He'd certainly been taught how to avoid being shot down, weaving right and left in the air.

The oil smell was getting stronger, but my sensors were still showing green on all counts, and I pressed forward. I didn't have infinite bullets, so I slowed my shooting to wait for a kill shot.

When it came, I didn't hesitate.

The engine smoked and the plane nosedived, headed toward a small, forested island rising out of the Madion Sea. I grinned in victory. There was no way he could survive a crash from that altitude.

Just as that thought floated through my head, a white parachute billowed out of the cockpit, and the princeling jumped out, hanging helplessly as the rest of his ship smashed nose-first onto the sandy beach of the island.

"No matter," I mumbled to myself, pulling out my gun again

and opening the small emergency hatch. I squinted as I aimed.

The bullet left the barrel but missed as my ship shuddered. The smell of burning oil was more pronounced now and I pulled the gun back in, banging my hand on my dashboard in the process.

To my horror, it unstuck all of the dials which tilted to their correct readings, telling me one thing: my ship was seconds away from exploding.

"No matter," I said, willing myself to be brave. I was going to kill the princeling before that happened.

I aimed at him, still wafting down to the island. I sent up a prayer and—

The engine exploded.

GALIAN

I swiveled my head around when I heard the huge explosion behind me. The plane smoked as it careened down to the island, where it sounded with a large *boom* that scared away a few flocks of birds. I wasn't sure what had happened, but I was thankful that the bad guy was no longer trying to kill me.

I landed with a soft *thump* on the sandy beach a little ways from my plane, and immediately dropped to my knees, releasing a loud breath. My hands shook and my heart pounded, but I thanked my lucky stars that I was *alive* and had practiced parachuting out of my plane a few extra times during my training.

Once my pulse returned to normal, I stood and released myself from the parachute straps, leaving the long trail of lines and white parachute laid out on the beach. I approached the wreckage of my plane. Pieces of it lay in a long trail as it had skidded across the sand. I picked up a metal piece that had a bullet hole in it and then tossed it aside.

Besides the nose and engine being smashed to smithereens, the back of the plane was fine. I cracked open the back hatch and pawed through my emergency supplies. I found everything—including the medical bag Dr. Maitland gave me—to be intact. Again, I thanked whatever was up there looking out for me. Of all the outcomes that could've happened from the battle, crash-landing on an island with my supplies was better than most.

A burning smell reached my nose, and I stepped back, searching my plane for any sign of fire. Then I noticed the black column of smoke rising up from the treetops.

Despite everything, worry knotted in my chest. What had happened to the other pilot? I hadn't seen another parachute. Was he even still alive? He was my enemy, but still a fellow human being. I couldn't help but hear Dr. Maitland in my ear.

I don't have the luxury of differentiating between Kylaen and Raven patients.

"Fuck him, he shot me down," I snapped to myself. Served him right if he burnt to a crisp.

I turned my head to look at the southern horizon, scanning the open blue sky for a plane or anyone who'd followed me. I was sure they would be there before sundown.

I mean, after all, I was a damned prince. My father would have to send for me.

I hoped.

Besides, there was no way they could miss the black smoke rising from the center of the island.

Guilt gnawed at me. I looked down at the medical bag and sighed. Dr. Maitland was right—I was a doctor first and a warrior second. Shouldering my bag, I stumbled off the sandy beach onto the firmer forest ground.

The trees were tall and thick and everything around me was green. It was late summer, but there was definitely a chill in the air since I was so far north. I was thankful for my extra layer under my jumpsuit.

I walked into a clearing, covering my nose from the smell. One of the two wings had been shorn off in the crash and was the source of the black smoke. The rest of the plane was mashed and mangled some ways away. I saw the pilot in the cockpit through the shattered glass, and his helmeted head hung motionless. I was sure that he was dead. I couldn't see how anyone could have survived such a crash.

And then he moved.

THREE

THEO

I woke slowly, the sound of unfamiliar animals coming to me first, followed by a cold breeze. As I tried to move, pain shot up from every corner of my body. I looked up at the blue sky, barely visible through a thick canopy of trees. I smelled leaking fuel, and wondered if my ship would explode or if I'd bleed to death first.

I relaxed into my seat and prepared for the inevitable. Even if the Raven government sent a search party for me (which they wouldn't), I doubted they'd come in time to save my life. Still, I took some solace in the fact that I killed another son of that God-damned mass murdering king.

A noise startled me and I turned my head slowly to find the source.

I couldn't believe my eyes. The stupid princeling was *alive* and standing in front of my ship.

Fear and anger gripped at me. How was it possible that I was badly injured and he appeared to be walking just fine? I hated that the last thing I was going to see in this world was Prince Galian standing in a clearing, his pale skin flushed and his eyes sparkling with...*amusement?*

I was dying and this son of a bitch was laughing at me.

"What's so funny?" I snarled through my helmet.

"Serves you right." He was smirking as if he had something to smirk about.

"For what?"

"Shooting me down. Looks like you're in worse shape than I am, too."

"Go to hell."

He laughed again and hoisted himself up onto the broken nose of my plane. I was in too much pain to fight back, and my gun was nowhere to be found.

"Yep," he observed, with a smirk on his face. Up close, he was every bit as handsome as I'd seen in pictures. "You definitely got what you deserved. Shouldn't have shot at me."

"You shouldn't have invaded my country."

His eyes widened for a moment and I thought I'd finally done something to wipe that smile off his face. To my supreme annoyance, he tilted his head back and let out a throaty laugh.

"Oh, you are witty," he said, nodding. "And technically right. But it wasn't my decision. I was, as they say, just following orders."

"And I was just following orders when I blew your ass out of the sky."

"Aren't we at an impasse then?" He seemed to be *enjoying* this conversation. He looked down at the side of my ship and read the inscription. "Theo, huh? Well, you must be a pretty high ranking pilot then. I hear the Ravens only allow you to put your name on your ship after you've survived plenty of battles."

I moved out of anger, but the pain in my legs came roaring up my body. "Please let me die in peace," I asked, unable to look at him.

"Oh, you aren't going to die today. But it would probably be safer if I pulled you out. I don't like the look of that fuel leak."

He leaned into my small cabin. If I'd had half a mind, I could've snapped his neck, but it was hard enough just to breathe. He found my seat strap and unhooked it, then lifted me out by my arms. I couldn't help but scream.

"Yeow, buddy," he said, stopping. He put one hand over his ear and muttered. "You sure got a girly scream."

"My legs are caught. Just leave me here. I'm as good as dead anyway."

"Naw, then who am I going to talk to while I wait to get picked up?" He sounded like he was waiting for dinner. "C'mon, we can get you out of here. Just take a deep breath. One...two..."

I didn't hear him count to three as he yanked my legs out of the mess and I screamed again, the pain so bad I almost lost consciousness. But, blessedly, it subsided, and the next thing I knew, he was laying me on the ground.

"There, now, Theo of Raven, let's take a look at you," he said, taking my helmet off.

GALIAN

Theo was a girl.

A pretty girl.

I'd always thought Raven women were more interesting

looking than Kylaen women—with their olive skin and black hair, they seemed to draw my attention. And this girl, something about her made my head spin.

Even with her mangled, bloody legs.

They were a sight: dark red staining her gray jumpsuit.

"Thank you, Dr. Maitland," I said, cracking open the bag he'd given me and sliding on the pair of latex gloves.

She murmured something. The amount of blood she'd lost was a real concern, and she was most likely concussed. I would worry about the head injury later; it wouldn't matter much if she died from blood loss.

"What are you doing?" she croaked.

"Pardon the invasion of privacy," I said, flashing her my trademark smile.

I unzipped her jumpsuit and pulled it down, exposing a white bra and underwear and nothing else. Immediately, her skin puckered with goosebumps as I tossed away the soaked dark gray suit.

"Are you still with me, Theo?"

She blinked, but didn't respond.

"Okay, I'm going to examine you now," I said, leaning over her bare legs. I pressed my hands to her hips, and she reacted, swiftly, sitting up so fast she nearly whacked her forehead to mine.

"*Get your filthy hands off of me*," she hissed, her breath touching my face.

"I'm a doctor."

"Bullshit."

"Seriously," I insisted. "You're bleeding very badly, and I need to find the source of it."

Her deep brown eyes stared into mine, her lip twisted in a

snarl, but she removed her hands from my wrists. I explored the bloody patches on her bare legs. Most of them seemed to be small scrapes...until I brushed something on the underside of her leg, and she screamed in pain.

"Ah, there it is," I said, placing my hand on her hip to calm her down. The four-inch gash was deep, and probably nicked an artery in the leg, based on the amount of blood seeping out of it.

Gently, I rolled her onto her stomach and she didn't protest. I used nearly every antibacterial wipe in the bag to clean the wound, then fished out sutures and twine.

"This is going to hurt," I said, sliding the needle through the bottom of the wound. She sucked in a loud breath, and her knuckles went white. I worked quickly, using all the sutures in the bag to close up the wound. I wrapped it with gauze as tightly as possible, hoping that it would keep her alive until we were found and I could get her to Dr. Maitland.

I rolled her back onto her back. She'd gone pale and was mumbling to herself. I fished out the tube and rubber tourniquet that I'd seen in the bag and looked at her.

"Well, Theo," I smirked. "You're just lucky I'm everybody's type."

"What are you doing?" she mumbled.

"Transfusion." I wrapped the rubber band tight around my forearm. Tying the other band around her arm, I felt for a vein—she was so muscular, it took me no time, and I stuck in the needle connected to the tube. With care, I slid the other end into my own vein and released the tourniquet.

She watched, wordlessly, as the red blood flowed from my arm down into hers. I counted the rate of blood flow on my watch.

"Okay," I said, sitting back and shaking my foggy head after I disconnected our transfusion line. There was significant bruising starting on her other leg on the inner calf, and it was swollen enough to make me curious.

"I'm going to check your leg," I said, placing my hand between her legs.

She tensed, and her eyes flew open.

"Theo," I said, as professionally as I could. "I think your leg is broken. I'm just going to check it. I promise, I'm not going to hurt you."

She snarled at me, but I continued moving my hands down to her knees and lower to her calves. She sucked in air when I touched the bruised spot, and, based on the swelling, I knew that if her tibia wasn't broken, it was close to it. At the very least, she needed a brace. Hopefully, there was something to help me in the bag. So far, Dr. Maitland hadn't let me down. I dug around for a moment, pulling out more antiseptic wipes and gauze, until my hands fell on a small box with a glass vial inside.

"You are one lucky girl," I said, assembling the needle. "This is anesthesia. It'll numb the pain locally until I can set the bone."

"I don't want your Kylaen poison," she spat, to my utter shock.

"Really?" I gaped at her. "I just gave you a damn liter of my own blood, and you think I'm going to *poison* you?"

She said nothing but looked away. Still muttering to myself about Raven paranoia, I pulled the cap off the syringe and inserted it into the swollen nub on her leg. She hissed, but I held still as I finished administering the drug. After a moment, she relaxed.

"Pain won't go away fully, and that's all that I have," I said. I glanced at the syringe and tossed it into a nearby bush, as I didn't have a biohazard disposal box at the ready. Then again, from the looks of this island, Theo and I seemed to be the only ones on it.

I stood up and looked around for a pair of sticks that would be sturdy enough to keep her from doing any more damage. I found a couple of straight ones that would do the trick and returned to her. She had regained a little color, and seemed to be enjoying the anesthesia because she seemed more relaxed when I crouched next to her.

She stared at the sky with a stoic resolve that I kind of admired. This girl was a warrior, having seen her share of scrapes and bruises, based on the state of her arms and legs. I was no longer surprised that she'd survived the crash of her ship.

What did surprise me was what she said when I finished bandaging her up.

THEO

"Thank you," I whispered, hating myself for uttering those words to a Kylaen. But this man—the *prince*—had not only bandaged me, but he'd given me some of his own blood, something I was still trying to wrap my head around. He'd said he was a doctor, and he ministered like one, but no word of this had reached Rave.

Doctor or not, I still wasn't sure what his intentions were. Perhaps they thought me a valuable prisoner of war, one they could torture into telling them the Raven military's secrets. Well, they would be in for a rude awakening. As if the Raven generals would tell a *kallistrate* anything.

He had disappeared again once he had finished binding my legs, but returned with a box and warm blanket. I hadn't even realized I was shaking, but it made sense. The northern Madion islands could get cold even in the summer months, and with my injuries, I was beginning to feel it.

"Here," the princeling said, unfolding the blanket and wrapping it around me with a gentleness that left me warm inside. "I'm worried you might go into shock, so you need to keep your body temperature up. Do you have any supplies on your ship?"

Supplies? What a laugh. Rave could barely afford to feed its own people, let alone put supplies on a ship that was more than likely going to be blown up.

He must've read my mind, because he thrusted the box in front of me. Inside were a few bags of food.

"This will have to do for today. But I'm hoping we'll be found before nightfall."

Ah, I thought, *so I was right*. He intended to bring me back as a prisoner of war.

"And if we aren't," he sighed, looking at the sky as if listening for the sound of jet engines, "we might just have to cuddle tonight, as that's my only blanket."

I bared my teeth at him. I *knew* he'd been trying to feel me up.

"Take your stupid blanket," I snapped, ripping it off and throwing it at him. I immediately missed the cover on my legs and I cursed my teeth for chattering.

"No, you need it more than I do," he said, picking it up off the ground and placing it over my bare, chilled legs. "I was mostly kidding about the cuddling thing, you know."

"You make too many jokes." I hated how much I loved this

blanket. This Kylaen blanket.

"That's what my father says, too." He smiled. "But when you're the youngest of three brothers, you make your own defense mechanisms."

I said nothing. If he was looking for pity from me, he was barking up the wrong tree.

"So, Theo. That's a boy's name, innit?"

I continued my silence.

"My mother wanted a girl," he said with a long sigh. "That's why they had three of us, you know. Though, my father was quite happy he had a spare second son!"

I looked up at him, unable to hide my surprise. He spoke about his dead brother with such nonchalance, such ease, that it made me question if he had a soul at all. It was no wonder his kind had no issues murdering us.

He sat down next to me, too close for my comfort, but seemed oblivious to everything.

"I didn't even *want* to be a pilot," he said, his voice softer. "I wanted to be a doctor. But after Dig died, my father basically forced me to join the military."

"Poor you." I remembered the day that the Raven military had come for me. I'd endured the first of many bruises that day.

"She speaks!" He grinned at me and my heart did the tiniest of flip-flops. If he hadn't been a Kylaen scumbag who I hated with every fiber of my being, I might've found him attractive, the way all my lieutenants did.

"Well, in any case, they should come find me soon," he said, scanning the sky again.

I scoffed, wrapping the blanket tighter around myself.

"You doubt Kylae's search and rescue forces?"

"On the contrary," I said, my voice laced with acid. "I fully expect them to find us within the day."

"So why the face?"

"I'm not looking forward to when they get here."

"Why?" he asked innocently.

"What do you think will happen when your rescuers arrive?" I spat at him. "I'm a *Raven soldier*. They're not just going to drop me off back in Vinolas! If I'm lucky, they'll just shoot me dead right here on this island."

He looked at me like he'd never considered his people might hurt me. How could he be so out of touch? Stupid princeling.

"I won't let them," he said, his face strange.

"If they don't shoot me, they're taking me back to Kylae," I said. "As a prisoner."

"They'll do neither of those things. You will be treated with respect like a human being."

I couldn't help the sardonic bark that came out. "You could win an award for naivety."

"It's not naivety! I'm the prince, and they'll do as I say."

No matter what he said, my fate was sealed. I wasn't making it off this island, and if they tried to take me, I would off myself before they had a chance to put me to work in one of their infamous death camps.

I stared into the woods. Why didn't I just slit my throat right there? If my death was an inevitability, why not take control and end it? The ultimate act of freedom and rebellion against Kylaen rule.

Selfishly, I knew why. I had grown quite accustomed to living and I wasn't too eager to give up the privilege. The small flame of hope that I could make it out alive was still there, the beacon of light that kept me moving. I'd survived the Raven military, I could survive this. It was possible, although improbable, that the Raven forces would find us first. Perhaps Lanis would pull some strings—I was a seven-year veteran of the force, a captain. Or perhaps they'd send out a search party. I wasn't ready to give up until I'd exhausted all my survival options. There was a chance, however small, that I could see my country again.

And if the Kylaen forces found me first, I'd deal with it at that point.

GALIAN

She was silent, but I could see worry etched on her face. In hindsight, telling her she'd be treated respectfully by my father's army did sound incredibly stupid and naive. She had just shot me out of the sky and tried to kill me. She was my enemy, and would probably slit my throat if she had the chance.

And yet, when I looked at her, I saw a human being. Flesh and blood with fears, hopes, dreams. She bled like any Kylaen patient I'd ever had. It was easy to pretend that the person in the other plane was a monster, but now, it was much harder when she was sitting there breathing next to me to wish for her death.

A loud grumbling interrupted my thoughts. After donating blood, I needed to eat soon or risk passing out.

I picked up the box of supplies and cracked it open, looking for anything decent to eat. I truly was not expecting to be there for long, but just in case, I wanted to spread out the rations as long as possible. A bag of nuts was my choice—protein and salt.

"Want one?" I offered to her.

In response, she pushed herself to her feet and hobbled away from me. I kept my seat, knowing she wasn't going to get far, especially since the anesthetic injection wasn't enough to dull the pain completely. As expected, she collapsed to the ground, and let out a long string of words I'd never heard before.

"What are you trying to do?" I called after her.

"Find shelter," she croaked back. "And water."

"I have water here," I said from my seat.

"Bully for you." I could tell she was in an immense amount of pain, and I couldn't help admiring her gumption.

"I meant, we can share it."

"It would probably kill me."

"Well, you look like you're about to die anyway, so why not go out in style?" I drawled, pushing the rest of the handful into my mouth. I was tired, and my blood sugar hadn't yet stabilized. And damn it, she was starting to piss me off. "For your last drink, why not drink some filtered Kylaen sweet water, instead of the chemically-laced shit you Ravens are forced to drink."

"Oh, go to *hell*," she hissed at me. "I'd rather drink my own piss than accept *anything* from you."

She pulled herself upright again and limped into the forest.

I sat there for a moment, angrily chewing on the peanuts and trying to keep myself seated. I owed her nothing, and she was being a real jackass about everything. Besides, it was *her* fault we were stuck there in the first place.

Still, I could hear Dr. Maitland in my ear, telling me it was my duty to get up and go after her. I was a doctor, she was my patient, and she was probably very scared right now. Not to mention concussed.

"Guh." I rolled my eyes and tossed the empty bag away. Pulling myself to my feet, I headed into the forest the way she went.

It didn't take me long to find her, curled up in a ball on the ground and crying in pain. A red stain was leaking through the binding around her thigh. She didn't even acknowledge my presence, but I kneeled down next to her anyway.

"So," I said gently, "you probably should stay put for a while, let that leg heal a little bit before you start walking on it."

"I'm as good as dead anyway," she whispered back. "I can't walk. I can't run. I have no food, no water, no shelter. And if the Kylaens find me first..."

"I'm not giving up, and neither should you." I grabbed her hand to pull her upright. It was small and cold, but mine was just as frigid. "I promise you, Theo of Raven, I am *not* going to let you die."

Disbelief was plain on her face, so I grasped her other hand.

"I give you my word, as Galian Neoptolemos Helmuth, third prince of the Kylaen nation, son of Grieg, that I will *not* let you die. All right?"

FOUR

THEO

I didn't trust the princeling, but I had no other options. I refused to let him carry me—although I was sure he would've had no problems with my small frame—so we hobbled back to where our supplies were, me on my good leg and leaning against him. He helped me sit back down on the ground against the tree. He wrapped the blanket around me and I had to admit, it felt nice to be warm again.

"Here," he said, unzipping his dark green uniform, revealing a thin white t-shirt and khaki pants underneath. He pulled it off and handed it to me.

"What?"

"You need it more than I do right now," he said. "We need to keep your body temperature up." He bent down and slid the soft material over my cold, bandaged legs. It was at least three sizes too big for me, and still warm from his body heat. I looked down at myself and nearly vomited at the sight of the Kylaen crest where the Raven one normally sat, and the name *Helmuth* in place of mine.

"Hey, it beats hypothermia," he said, noticing the look on my face as he tossed the blanket back over my legs.

I nodded and pulled the blanket higher, covering up the offending patches. "Are you even a doctor?"

"Yes," he said, looking perplexed. "I thought it was pretty common knowledge that I graduated from medical school?"

"Was that between your socialite girlfriends and embarrassing debauchery?"

His eyebrows shot up so fast I thought they might leave his face, and a small blush appeared on his pale cheeks. "I... Yes, I am a doctor," he said after stammering for a few moments. The blush deepened and he spun around to look toward the forest. He mumbled something about going to his ship then disappeared through the trees.

Even though I was in pain and still lightheaded from the ordeal, I couldn't help the smile twisting the corners of my mouth. He was every bit the spoiled brat that I had pictured him to be—supposed medical training aside—and it pleased me to get the better of him. It was a small Raven victory against the Kylaen royal family.

And yet...I could land an even stronger blow if I simply killed him.

After all, if by some miracle the Raven forces found us first, they might have some questions about why Prince Galian wasn't, well...*dead* by my hand. They wouldn't care that he'd saved my life; rather, they would've expected me to give my life in pursuit of our independence as long as I took the princeling out with me.

For some reason, I couldn't see myself ending his life there on the island. I couldn't count how many Kylaens I'd shot down over the years, but the prospect of taking a human life when it was sitting next to me? The thought made me queasy. It seemed my humanity was overpowering my Raven pride.

And of course, my injury was quite severe, as I was reminded when I tried to move. A broken leg was definitely troublesome, and limited my movement and ability to fend off predators. I had no idea where my pistol was, and even if I found it, I was most likely running low on bullets.

Bullets, I reminded myself, that I'd used to try to kill the man who'd saved my life.

My ship was still smoldering in the clearing nearby, twisted beyond recognition. Thanks to the princeling's blood transfusion, my mind was clearer and I saw how close I had come to my own end. Perhaps there was still more for me to do before I moved to the next life.

That is, if I made it off this island.

The princeling returned from his ship with two more water bottles in his hands. He seemed to have walked off whatever embarrassment he felt from my comments on his party-boy past had caused, as he smiled handsomely and handed me one of them.

"As promised, Miss."

"Captain," I responded, taking the water and sipping it. I'd worked too hard for my rank to not be addressed by it.

"Captain, my apologies." He took a seat next to me, gulping his water without any concern for rationing, staring up at the sky and expecting Kylaen ships to appear at any second.

But enough time had passed that if they had been close behind him, or known where he had crashed, they would have been there already. There was the distinct possibility that we would be spending the night, and based on the sun's position in the sky, I knew it was better if we prepared than be caught off guard.

"So, Princeling..."

"I'm sorry, what?" He blinked at me.

"Princeling." The horrified look on his face tugged a smile onto my lips. "It's what we call you in Rave."

"I have a name, you know," he said, turning to look at me superiorly.

"I'm not calling you *Your Highness*," I spat at him.

"That's not my name either. It's Galian."

"Whatever," I huffed, vowing *never* to call him by anything other than princeling. "We might want to consider that we won't be found today."

"Do you think?" he asked, giving me a curious look.

"I think we're at least a couple hundred miles away from either Kylae or Rave," I said calmly. "I think there are a smattering of islands this far north, and planes or ships only rarely come up here. It may take the Kylaen forces some time to comb through all the possible areas you *could* have landed in—"

"You don't think the Raven forces will find us first?" he asked. "You're a captain, aren't you? Surely they'll send out a search party."

I bit my tongue as I wondered how to respond. Would it be devastating to our national security to tell him that we barely had the resources to defend our shores, let alone send out a search party for one wayward pilot? To be safe, I decided against answering his question at all.

After a moment of silence, he half-smiled. "Well, that's good news for me, I guess. I'm sure they'd have a field day if they found *me* here."

"Back to the issue at hand," I said, not wanting to dwell on Raven forces finding the princeling alive. "We should make preparations for tonight before it gets dark. How much food is in your box there?"

He glanced inside and poked around. "Probably enough for the two of us for one night."

"Good, and I would ration your water as well." I nodded to the bottle in his hand. "Until we can find more drinkable water, that is. Or I can make some from the sea water."

He stared at me with a blank expression. "How long are you planning on us being here?"

"We need to gather wood for a fire," I said instead of answering his question. "And see if we can find some shelter. It's not too cold now but once it gets dark, we'll need to be protected." I shifted and winced at the pain. "And unfortunately, I'm not going to be much help to you."

"No, you sit here," he said, popping up. With a grin, he added, "Doctor's orders."

"Gather kindling and bigger logs as well. We'll need enough to last us through the night." I was beginning to feel more comfortable as I approached our present situation as I did a flight mission. With the princeling healthy and his ship full of supplies to last us at least until the morning, things didn't look quite as grim. "What other supplies are on your ship?"

"I-I don't know," he stammered.

"Gather whatever we can from your ship and bring it here so we can see what we have and what we'll need to," I grimaced, looking at the wilderness around us, "figure out."

"Just in case," he added, and for the first time, I heard his nerves.

GALIAN

"Just in case," she confirmed, but I didn't hear the conviction I was looking for. For some reason, Theo thought we were going to be there a while. It unsettled me.

But she was right. With only a few hours before the sunlight was gone, it was better to be safe than sorry.

I think she took some pleasure in barking orders at me as I set up our makeshift camp—building a fire, checking all our supplies, using our one blanket as a small tent. Theo seemed to be regaining her faculties which made me less concerned that she had a concussion. She also wasn't suffering any adverse effects from the blood transfusion, so I didn't mind that she corrected almost everything I did.

"Not like that," she huffed, hobbling over to the pile of leaves I was trying to light on fire. She wouldn't accept my hand to help her sit, instead falling hard on her broken leg and hissing loudly. She seemed to get over it quickly, leaning forward to hit the two stones together harder than I was. In almost no time, the dry leaves were smoking.

"Thanks," I said, dumbly watching the kindling wither and die. She ignored me in favor of tending to the fire. "I usually have people do that." I laughed, trying to cut the silence with my awkward brand of humor.

She paused, and a look flitted across her face: a mixture of disgust and hatred. Not one I was used to seeing from a woman, especially when I reminded them of my status. Obviously, being royalty wasn't going to get me very far with this girl.

When the fire was a healthy size, I felt confident enough to take the stick from her. "You need to rest. Doctor's orders."

She snorted derisively.

"Problem?"

"I can't believe *you're* qualified to give medical advice," she muttered.

"Now hold on a second," I said, letting my voice raise in anger. "I spent four years in the Royal Kylaen University medical program and was about to start my residency when..."

She turned to look at me when I trailed off.

"When my *father* pulled me out," I finished darkly.

"For embarrassing the country?"

"No, actually, because you guys blew my older brother out of the sky, and he wanted me in the military. So, *Captain*, I suggest you quit the smart-ass remarks." I finally felt like I had the upper hand. She clammed up, but that self-satisfied smirk remained on her face. She was infuriating but...also alluring; I always had a thing for women who weren't afraid of me. And it had not escaped my notice that she and I were the only ones there, and we could find lots of fun ways to stay warm.

But I kept that thought to myself. She'd probably sever my manhood if I broached the subject.

"What are you looking at?" she asked, noticing my stare.

"I...uh...curious about your injuries," I said, scrambling for an excuse that wasn't what I was actually thinking. "How is your head, any pain?"

"Not as much as the one in my ass." She'd meant to say it under her breath, but I heard it.

I narrowed my eyes at her. "Remember, I can take back my

jumpsuit at anytime, *Captain.*"

"I suggest you pay more attention to your own pants," she said with a smile.

I looked down and jumped three feet; in my attentiveness to her, my pant leg had ventured too close to the fire and caught. With a hiss, I patted it out and sniffed at my singed hem.

"What did you do with my jumpsuit, anyway?" she asked.

"Over there," I said, nodding to the pile of bloody clothes on the other side of the camp. "It was pretty torn up. Mine seems to be a little thicker and warmer."

She glanced down at the name on her chest and grimaced again. "I'd rather freeze to death than wear this. If your soldiers come, I don't want them confusing me for a Kylaen."

Her pride in her country was incredible. I never thought someone could be so thickheadedly loyal to something. "There's no way you could pass for a Kylaen. I think you bleed black and gold."

I was pleased at the smile that appeared on her face. Maybe I was growing on her after all.

THEO

I prayed that my last days in this world would not be filled with the princeling's terrible sense of humor. His superiority was disgusting, and his attempts to remind me of his status as a royal only served to make me wish I had the nerve to kill him.

"So...tell me about yourself."

I glanced over at the princeling across the fire. "This isn't a date."

"No, because if it were, I doubt I'd choose someone with such a piss-poor attitude, but here we are."

I had to give him credit; he had some bite to him. "What do you want to know?"

"For starters, what's your name?"

"Theo."

"That's not your name," he scoffed. "That's...a nickname or—"

"Theo Kallistrate," I said, not bothering to explain to him what *kallistrate* meant in the old Raven language. I doubt he knew anything about my country, seeing as his father was intent on wiping it out.

"But Theo's a guy's name." He seemed preoccupied with this fact. "I mean, are you trying to pretend to be a guy for military purposes or—"

"That is the name they gave me at the orphanage and that is the name I use," I said, hoping the conversation would end.

Unfortunately, it didn't. "You're an orphan?"

I closed my eyes and sighed. "Yes."

"Did you even know your parents?"

"No."

"Really?"

"Princeling, if you're going to doubt everything I tell you, why ask at all?"

"Why do you keep calling me that?" he asked. To my pointed look, he added, "I won't doubt what you say."

"Because you're the...princeling," I said with a small shrug. "You aren't the heir, and you aren't the military hero. You're just..."

"I see," he said. "So I'm a big joke to you guys too, huh?"

"The tabloid stories didn't help."

"Oh son of a... It was like, *twice*!" he exclaimed, his voice echoing in the clearing. "I'm not allowed to make a mistake *twice*?"

I wondered if I should contradict him, seeing as our lucky wall back in Rave had no less than six separate instances of public intoxication, and, at last count, ten different girls. But I decided against it, seeing as he was arguing with me anyway.

"And I suppose you've never made a mistake in your entire life?" he asked me.

"Not one that made the papers."

He snorted and grumbled under his breath. At least he had the decency to be embarrassed. If his claims about his medical degree were true, then perhaps he was trying to make a change for the better.

But the conversation was making my head ache—I needed peace and quiet, and the sun was starting to set.

"It would probably be best if we took turns staying up and guarding the campsite from predators," I said. "So one of us should sleep now." *You, please.*

"Predators?" He nervously glanced into the darkening woods. "You think?"

"I think we should prepare for all possibilities." I shifted and nodded towards the makeshift tent. "You sleep now. I'm used to staying up all night anyway."

"Why?"

I wished I hadn't said anything. I had made a habit of staying up to watch over the newer female pilots so that the male ones wouldn't bother them, like some of the older girls had done for me when I was a kid. But I didn't want to tell the princeling anything about Rave. I just wanted him to shut up and let me think.

"Go to sleep, princeling," I snapped, hoping it would end the conversation.

"You know," he said, standing up and walking over to the tent. "If we're gonna be stuck here, you might have to suffer and talk to me for more than two minutes." And with that, he lay down away from me, and quieted.

I glared at his back for a moment, and then the reality of our situation came to me. I was trapped on a deserted island with the Prince of Kylae, without whom I would be dead. And by some cruel twist of fate, we were dependent on each other. He was useless as he was, and I was useless with my injury. But our supplies would not last through another day, and it was imperative that we work together to secure food, shelter, and water.

I glanced at the half-empty water bottle and grimaced. Unless I could find a fresh water pond somewhere (doubtful), I would have to figure out how to desalinate the seawater. Somewhere in the back of my memory, I knew the basic principles of evaporation and condensation, but finding the right tools would be the challenge.

Without the incessant yapping of the princeling, I could hear the quiet forest, the far off lapping of the sea waves against the beach, the sound of small bugs chirping and sleep pulled at me.

GALIAN

Was I slightly nervous to be exposing my back to a Raven soldier? I'm not going to lie and say I was completely okay with it. After a while, I relaxed. But I did not sleep.

The day's events finally came washing over me in a delayed-response slow motion. From my first air battle to being shot out of the sky to finding Theo nearly dead in her ship. And I'd saved her, I'd given her my *blood*, the very same person who'd tried to kill me. And now we were stuck on this island together, relying on each other to make it until morning, or until the Kylaen air patrol found us.

I mulled her words. She was so sure the Kylaens would be the aggressors, shooting her on sight or taking her prisoner. Did she really have such a low opinion of my people?

This girl, this pilot, this soldier, she was an enigma to me. I had never met another person—female or otherwise—so intense and closed off. Every move she made seemed to be a calculation of her survival rate, and the odds never seemed to be in her favor. Rave was a hard country to grow up in, but to see one of its citizens up close, made it clear just how hard it was for them.

My pity for her grew as I thought about all the hardships she must have endured to get to this point. And yet, for all her gruffness, I *did* think she had a good soul, somewhere deep down.

When I turned over to glance back at her, she'd nodded off. I sat up and shook my head. So she wasn't completely infallible after all. I walked over and crouched down in front of her, waiting for her to wake up and bark some derogatory order at me. When she didn't even flinch, I gathered her in my arms and carried her to the makeshift shelter. After I laid her down, she curled into a ball, looking much calmer, and more peaceful than she had all day.

Desperately wishing for coffee or a book or something to pass the time, I settled for sitting next to the fire and watching this enigmatic Raven girl sleep.

FIVE

GALIAN

I was cold, and also very uncomfortable. For a brief moment, I'd thought that I had been in my bed, perhaps having tossed the covers off of me and the window left open. But no, I opened my eyes, I was outside, sleeping next to a tree, a mostly dead fire smoldering in front of me and a Raven girl sleeping soundly next to me and wearing my jumpsuit.

Theo hadn't moved since I placed her there the night before. I probably needed to check her thigh and the rest of her injuries again, to make sure they weren't infected. But if I tried to get close to her in her sleep, she'd probably choke me.

I sighed loudly. I wanted a shower and I wanted my morning breakfast delivered to my room with a piping hot pot of coffee. There couldn't be much food left, which meant that if someone didn't find us soon—

Somewhere in the back of my head, I registered a buzzing sound.

A buzzing.

A *buzzing*.

A plane.

I was on my feet in a moment, sprinting toward the beach before I even realized what was going on. Exhilaration pulsed through me as I dashed over foliage and tree branches. I burst onto the beach and there was my ride home. A small metal tube glinting in the sunlight, buzzing around above us.

"*Hey!*" I screamed, waving my arms wildly, but I knew I was just a speck on the ground. I dashed over to my ship and dug through the supplies. My hopes soared when I found a flare gun.

I stepped away from the plane, squinting in the bright sky. A flare might not be visible. The plane was flying away so I had to think fast.

Theo's ship! It had been leaking fuel the day before, and would most assuredly catch fire. Dashing back through the forest, I prayed and hoped and begged whatever deity was up there to let the plane stay near. I ran into the clearing, aimed the flare gun, and fired.

The explosion was massive and instant, a fireball that plumed from the fuselage into the sky. I held my breath and—

"*What the hell did you do?*"

I spun around. Theo was awake, her face pale and her eyes glued on what was left of her plane.

"There was a plane," I stammered, taken aback by the shock on her face. "It's coming...or..."

I looked up at the sky, horribly devoid of the plane I had seen moments earlier. I was too late—even though this pile of metal was billowing black smoke high into the sky, it wasn't enough.

"*Shit,*" I hissed kicking the ground.

A sobbing sound drew my attention from the sky. Theo had

fallen to her knees, staring at the burning wreckage with her jaw open and tears—real, thick, honest tears—slipping down her cheeks.

THEO

My eyes were glued to the flaming wreckage. I sank to my knees and tears fell down my face.

"What's wrong?" he asked. "Are you hurt?"

"Y-you blew up my ship..."

"I thought I heard a plane." He sounded disappointed and infuriatingly unconcerned that he had destroyed the only thing I had ever called mine. I didn't care that she wouldn't fly, she was still my girl. "Are you sure you're okay?"

"Of course I'm not okay. You *blew up my ship*."

"You're getting all worked up over a stupid *plane*?"

If I spent one more minute in his presence, I was going to rip his stupid head off. "*Can you give me a moment?*" I spat through bared teeth.

"*Really?*" he asked, sounding genuinely shocked. "You're an odd one, Theo."

I didn't expect him to understand, but was grateful that he walked away at that moment. I waited until the sound of his steps disappeared before the floodgates opened.

Letting my tears fall onto my knees, I thanked my ship for the five years she'd served me faithfully. She had protected me against Kylaen bullets, and had been the only thing I could count on in this world. Without her, I felt abandoned, like the *kallistrate* I was.

I punched the ground, my wails growing louder. Why was life so unfair? Why had I been born a Raven, doomed to serve as a slave my entire life? Why hadn't I just died in the crash?

Sitting on the ground, I wallowed in my misery and the uncertainty of my fate. I was even less in control of my life on this island, and it was suffocating.

I wasn't sure how long I watched my ship burn, but by the time the flames died down to small flickers, my desolation had turned to fury. I convinced myself that I could have fixed my ship, given enough time. But now, all that was left was a hunk of metal. Useless, just like me. Just like that stupid son of a bitch who'd set my ship on fire.

I *hated* him even more than I had before. I wished with all my being that I had killed him when I had the chance. I wanted to rip off this disgusting jumpsuit with the vile Kylae crest and his repulsive name sewn onto the other side. *Helmuth*, the name of the king. The man who sent his minions to decimate my people, who continued this pointless war just to reclaim his glory.

And now his disgraceful son had taken the one thing I'd ever called mine.

"How ya doing?"

I clenched my jaw. "Don't talk to me."

"C'mon Theo, I was just trying to get us rescued! That was a hunk of junk. It wasn't gonna fly again—"

Rage screamed out of me. I needed to get away, far away, before I became a murderer on top of everything else. I began walking as fast as my broken leg could take me.

"You know what? *Fine*," he barked after me. "If you want to wander off on your own and get yourself killed, you go ahead and do that! You seem to have a death wish anyway!"

I hobbled until the pain in my leg overpowered my fury, and I collapsed on the ground, looking up at the gray sky and gritting my teeth in pain. I wasn't sure how far I had traveled, but I hoped it was far enough to hide me if his army showed up. Maybe if they found him, they wouldn't comb the island for me. Maybe I could just survive there like a wild woman.

I sat up and crawled to a nearby tree, sitting against it as my leg throbbed. I quieted my sobs and wiped my wet face, calming myself down.

Embarrassment began to set in as I considered the facts. My ship really was never going to fly again and it was awfully smart of him to try and get their attention. And, yet again, my injuries were so severe that it didn't do me any favors to make an enemy of the only other person on this island.

I tried to get up and hissed loudly at the sharp pain from my leg. As soon as I could pull myself up, I would apologize.

Unable to move, I distracted myself with the sounds of the island. The chirping birds were a good sign; at least there was meat on this barren hunk of land. Catching them would be a conundrum for another day.

The bushes in front of me rustled. To my complete shock and surprise, a rabbit appeared. Two ears, puffy tail. Big, twitching eyes.

How the hell had a rabbit gotten onto this island?

I moved, scaring it back into the recesses of the thick brush from whence it came. Were my eyes playing tricks on me? Or had my earlier hysteria caused some kind of a hallucination?

I heard more movement behind me, and figured it must be the princeling come to retrieve me back to camp.

"Princeling, I—"

A low growl answered me, one that was decidedly not human. Slowly, I looked behind the tree.

Shaggy coat, big, gleaming eyes, and razor-sharp teeth dripping with drool.

A wolf.

GALIAN

I sat on the beach, gazing at the sky, trying to will my blood pressure to return to normal after Theo and the plane. That couldn't have been the only plane. They had to come for me.

Still, somewhere in the back of my mind, I was worried. My mother would move heaven and earth to find me, but my father? Not so much. He might actually be happy if I died in battle, the same way Digory had.

But they'd pulled his body out of the floating wreckage in the south Madion sea. They'd seen him go down, saw him hit the water. How many precious war-focused resources would be used to locate my body?

"Please don't leave me here," I said, hoping my words would fly across the ocean to someone's ears. The wreckage was still smoldering, and a trail of smoke billowed overhead.

I looked down at the flare gun in my hand. I had two more flares in the box, so I loaded one in the empty barrel and kept the second in my pocket. I removed the rest of the supplies from the ship, just in case, and left them on the beach.

Once that was finished, I stood on the beach and stared into the woods, glaring at the direction Theo had left in. She was being a real bitch. So what if I'd blown up her plane? It was nothing but a hunk of metal anyway, and she was stupid to think that she would've been able to fix it.

And she was even more stupid for wandering off by herself.

Again.

I probably would find her curled up in a ball, crying.

Her wound probably reopened.

She'd bleed out if I didn't tend to it quickly.

Again, Dr. Maitland's words echoed in my head. How many patients had he calmly tended to over the years who'd been obstinate and rude? And yet, he'd continued to treat them with respect and kindness.

The man was obviously a saint.

And he would be disappointed in me if I let her die.

"*Fine*!" I barked, kicking the sand.

THEO

I stared into the eyes of the wolf, frozen with fear. There was nothing I could do. Couldn't run, couldn't hide. I was sure it could smell the blood on my leg, and I was also sure that the beast thought me to be an easy meal.

Oh God, I was going to die.

Staring at the white-toothed, quite possible painful death in front of me, I realized very acutely that I wasn't ready to die.

It crept closer and closer. I clawed at the ground, searching for anything that would help me in a fight. The only things my fingers ran over were small twigs and pebbles, nothing of any use against a ninety-pound wolf.

"Stay?" I whispered, knowing that it was useless.

The wolf crouched, and I closed my eyes. This was it. I steeled myself for the pain.

And nearly pissed myself when a loud crack echoed in the clearing.

My eyes flew open and I smelled the acrid remnants of gunpowder. The wolf was gone, no doubt scared off by the sound. My gaze landed on the princeling, holding the flare gun and looking about as shocked as I felt.

I tore my eyes away from him and stared at the spot where the wolf had been, my heart still beating out of my chest. I was aware of the princeling walking over to me, but I didn't want him to be a party to my reacquaintance with my own mortality.

He didn't seem to get the message, standing too close to me and then bending down to get a better look at me. He stood back up and looked at his flare gun as he reloaded it nonchalantly.

"Only got one left."

"That's it?" I snapped, expecting him to say something else, although I wasn't sure why I expected it or what I needed him to say.

He blinked in confusion. "What's it?"

"You saved my life," I blurted. "Twice..." I looked up at the sky in shock. "*Why?*"

"I have no idea." He shrugged. "Maybe I'm just a decent human being. And maybe I don't want to be stuck here on this islan.. myself."

I swallowed.

"C'mon," he approached me and offered his hand. "We need to stay close to camp. I can carry you back."

But I wouldn't move, I just kept staring at him.

"Theo?"

"You've saved my life twice now," I said, looking up at him. "And I hate being in Kylaen debt. So I...we need to make it even. Or at least...more even..."

"Wow," he said with a barking laugh. "Well, then, I guess you'll have to tell me some deep, dark Rave state secret."

He was clearly being sarcastic, but I didn't care. I needed to level things out now. Raven tradition dictated it; soldiers always wanted to be *niec*, or square.

After a moment, I replied with the only state secret I knew: "Theophilia."

"What?"

"My full name is Theophilia Kallistrate."

"Theophilia Kallistrate, hm?" he rumbled, rubbing his chin. "So I save your life twice and you tell me your real name?" He paused. "Seems fair."

I folded my arms across my chest. "Well, if the opportunity presents itself for me to save your life," I allowed myself to smile at him, "I shall return the favor."

"How about you start with letting me carry you back to camp?"

SIX

GALIAN

We walked back to camp with the tension eased between us. She no longer seemed to hate every fiber of my being, even going so far as to apologize for the way she'd reacted. I wasn't quite sure why she had become so overly emotional about her plane, but I did know she'd tell me if she wanted to.

We spent the rest of the day in the campsite, and I was starting to get antsy. It had been nearly twenty-four hours since we'd crashed and besides that one plane, no one had come for us. Our water was running low, so Theo'd sent me back to the wreckage of my ship to retrieve some metal pieces that she could use to make a double boiler. I returned with three pieces—two large curved metal facing from my wing, a smaller one that could fit inside.

Theo directed me to place one of the pieces over the fire, then to return to the ocean and fill one of our now-empty water bottles with seawater. When I returned, she'd placed one of the larger pieces over the fire, and settled the smaller piece in the center.

"I need two large sticks," she said, taking the water from me.

I left and picked out two sturdy branches nearby. When I returned, she'd emptied the sea water into the bottom of the larger curved metal piece.

"Cut those in half," she ordered. "Then stick them in the ground here."

I did as she asked and helped her place the larger piece on top of the sticks, suspending the third curved piece on top. We waited for a moment, holding our breath, but the structure held.

"Go back and get more," she said, thrusting the plastic bottle at me again. I held in my comment about asking nicely and retrieved more water. She sent me on this errand five more times before she was satisfied.

"So what is this thing?" I asked.

"The water boils on the bottom piece," she said, pointing to the sizable water that had begun to steam. "The top piece collects the condensation. It drips into the bowl. Clean water."

"Wow," I said, sitting back. "I never would've thought of that. Did they teach you that in flight school?"

She clenched her jaw, either deep in thought or ignoring me, so we sat and watched the sea water bubble and steam for a while. The water was slow to boil, slow to condense on the top layer, and even slower to drip. This process was going to take a long time. I was already thirsty.

"Princeling."

"What?"

"You saw that wolf, right?"

"The one about to eat you? Sure."

She half-cracked a smile. "How did a wolf get on this island?"

I opened my mouth then closed it. "That's a good question.

Wolves don't just appear on islands hundreds of miles from the mainland. They can't swim that far."

"Right before it showed up, I thought I saw a rabbit, too," she said.

"A rabbit?" I laughed. "Furry tail?"

"If I didn't imagine that wolf, I didn't imagine the rabbit either." She chewed on her lip. "So the question is how?"

"Does it matter?" I asked.

"It matters if one rabbit happened to appear on this island, or a whole population. Do you want to eat tomorrow?" She nodded to the open box of supplies, and I tried not to think about how low it was. "That'll be a lot easier if there's ample meat roaming around here."

Tomorrow, and the next day, and the next day—Theo's concern was for a much longer term than I'd considered. She seemed to think that we would be there for a while, and for whatever reason, the implications of that finally sank in.

The remains of my ship were visible on the beach, and anyone truly looking for me would have seen it. If they'd noticed it, they would have already sent soldiers to come get me. They had no idea Theo was there, with her knowledge of how to construct a double boiler to capture drinking water or else we'd be dead from dehydration before we could starve. God forbid she suffer from infection from her wound and die. Then I'd really be in trouble. I had no idea how to hunt or to catch food. I didn't know which plants were poisonous and which were safe. I'd gotten lucky with that wolf earlier, what would happen when the entire pack showed up?

All of which served to point out, very clearly, what my father had been trying to tell me for years: I was completely and totally useless.

What use were all the skills learned at the Royal Kylaen Academy on this island? I couldn't even take care of myself. Sure I could wrap a tourniquet and administer antibiotics. I could even assist in surgery should the situation call for it. I could get a plane in the air and get it back on the ground.

But, as His Highness said, that was worthless when it came to battle. I was there to kill people, not save them.

I would never forget him after Digory's death. My mother had been inconsolable for days. Although she hadn't had as close a bond with him as with me, he was still her son. But my father was nearly over the moon with pride that his son had died in his war. Digory wasn't even cold in the ground before he began suggesting I do the same.

Now there I was, marooned on an island in the northern Madion Sea, and he probably figured if I wasn't dead already, I would be soon. That meant he could plaster my face on the screens in every home in Kylae. He could re-galvanize our troops to take revenge against Rave. He'd use my death as reason to continue the bloodshed.

Which meant no one was coming for me.

And I suddenly became scared.

THEO

When I awoke, the princeling was nowhere to be found, but he had left the flare gun at my fingertips. Still, after our encounter with the wolves, it was odd for him to venture far away from camp. He had been quiet last night; there was something different about him I couldn't figure out.

I tried to get up, but my leg was stiff and painful. I rubbed the sore spot gingerly. The nub of broken bone beneath the skin had formed a knot under the cotton of the princeling's uniform. My injury would certainly put a damper on our survival chances, but with the princeling completely healthy, I could rely on him to do most of the manual labor.

A noise in the brush interrupted my thoughts and I nearly fired the flare gun, until I saw it was simply the princeling returning from the beach. Pale-faced and peaky from the wind, he wore a grim expression. Without a word to me, he walked over to the box of supplies we had been slowly eating through. I knew what he was going to say before he said it.

"We're out of food."

I nodded, rubbing my hands in front of the small fire to warm up.

"We're going to die here, aren't we?" he whispered weakly.

The sudden lack of food seemed to have panicked him. Can't say I blame him; if I'd grown up in a castle with glittering buffets every night, I would be concerned after the first day of without food as well.

"You don't think they're coming for you?" I asked, instead of answering his question. "You're a prince of Kylae."

It was his turn not to answer my question, as his face turned upwards toward the sky. There was obviously something he didn't want me to know, but it was etched all over his face. He thought the plane yesterday was a fluke. For some reason, he felt the Kylaen forces weren't searching for him.

As well as that boded for my survival chances, it wasn't good news for our non-existent supplies.

"Then I suppose we should start setting some traps," I said, cutting the silence between us.

"Traps?"

"For food."

"O...okay." He nodded dumbly but didn't move.

"We need to search for better shelter," I said. "Which means I'll have to stay here and set traps while you—"

"I won't even know what to look for, Theo."

It was clear how far he'd sunk into despair. I needed him to be lucid, as eager to live as I was. With a grimace, I forced myself into Captain Kallistrate. He was just another of my lieutenants, green and scared.

"We have everything we need," I said. "We just need to think rationally—find shelter, trap some food."

"What's the point?"

"Galian." It was the first time I had ever used his name, and it got his attention. "I know it looks bleak, but I've been through bleaker situations, and I'm still here. You and I wouldn't have survived the crash just to die here, all right? I don't think God has such a sick sense of humor."

He swallowed and looked at the ground, regaining some of his color. "I didn't take you for a spiritual person, Theo."

"I..." I looked away. "I have to believe that there's something out there that's in control here. Because why would we survive a crash and," I chuckled, "survive *each other* just to die here? It doesn't make sense."

"Do you really believe that?"

"I believe that right now we can't focus on what might or might not happen. These are the facts of the situation—we need to eat and we need shelter. Once we get those two things figured out...then we can think about the rest of it."

The smallest of laughs rumbled in his chest. "So which do you want to do first, Captain?"

My stomach growled, answering his question.

GALIAN

Theo continued to impress me. Her pep talk about God had made it clear she was used to commanding troops. Most impressive was the rudimentary trap that she had concocted. She had me dig a hole in the ground with my hands then cover it with sticks and leaves. I doubted it would work. An hour later, I was even more doubtful, and starting to get cranky from low blood sugar.

"I think we need to consider another option."

"Ssh," she whispered, gaze pinned on the forest.

Then, as if from a dream, a rabbit appeared in the woods, just as Theo had said. We had left a few empty wrappers of my food rations on top of the trap as a lure, and the rabbit seemed curious enough to take the bait. I heard Theo hold her breath beside me, and I kept mine as well, waiting as it inched closer and closer and...

"*Get it!*" Theo bellowed at me as soon as the white tail disappeared through the hole.

I sprang to my feet in an instant and ran over. It struggled in the trap, hopping and jumping, and I picked it up gingerly. It was so cute and fluffy that I suddenly forgot my hunger.

"Bring it here," Theo said.

"I...No."

She looked at me like I had two heads. "And why not?"

"We can't, Theo, it's so cute—"

"And what do you think pork looks like?" she deadpanned. "Would you like to eat or would you like to starve to death?" She took a long breath. "I promise you, where there's one, there's probably a thousand more that look just like him. If we're lucky."

I swallowed and brought the struggling creature over to her. She took it from my hand and, before I could look away, snapped its poor little neck with a sickening crack.

"God, Theo!" I hissed at the limp body now hanging by its ears. "Give me some warning next time, will you?"

"It didn't feel anything," she said as if she were talking about a stuffed animal. "Let's get back to camp so we can have some breakfast."

I took the still-warm rabbit from her with a grimace, but Theo ignored it as she climbed onto my back so I could carry her to camp. It was the quickest way, we'd figured, to travel around the island. Although it was a little unnerving having her hands, which had so easily snapped the neck of the rabbit hanging so near my own.

Back at camp, Theo slid off my back with the rabbit in hand. She hobbled over to the pile of supplies and produced a knife. And without warning (again), she sliced into the rabbit.

"Ugh, Theo." I winced. "Warning."

"Aren't you a doctor?" she asked me, ignoring the blood that splattered on her face.

She cut the meat as if she knew what she was doing. I couldn't help remembering some of the Raven horror stories Dig used to tell me as a child. He said the Raven military sliced up their prisoners and ate them because they didn't have enough food over there. I knew it was bullshit, but something about the way she expertly moved the knife was disconcerting, especially after she'd killed it so carelessly.

"Where did you learn to do that?" I asked.

"Killing Kylaen soldiers."

"Oh God." I looked away, suddenly sick.

"I'm kidding," she said with the smallest of laughs. "There was a butcher shop down the road from the orphanage, and some of the kids were sent to work there since..." She must have realized she'd said something too revealing about Rave, because she trailed off and worked with more vigor.

"So how long did you work for the butcher?" I asked.

"Until I was conscripted."

I almost didn't want to know the answer, but I asked, "And how old were you then?"

Another hard slice as she hit bone. "Twelve."

I blew out between my lips. Rave and their stupid conscription. I eyed her, trying to place her age. She acted much older than I did, but looked less than twenty.

"I'm nineteen now," she answered my unasked question.

"Seven years in the Raven military," I observed.

"You don't make captain unless you're brought in that way or you've put in your time," she said proudly. "I was promoted last year."

"Why's it so hard?" I asked. In Kylae, our soldiers were promoted from lieutenant to captain without much fuss or difficulty. I was a captain, if memory served, but I'd started as a lieutenant last year.

Her face had turned stony again, as she considered whether or not to answer me. "Because most of us don't survive that long."

The weight of her statement sucked the air from my chest. Theo suddenly made sense to me. She'd never known anything other than a soldier's life. Surviving marooned on a deserted island was nothing compared to what she had gone through before. She hadn't simply been waxing poetic when she spoke about God's purpose—it was the basis for her survival. She had no control over her own life, so she placed it in someone else's hands, and hoped for the best.

She'd stuck the pieces of meat on some sticks and placed them over the fire. Now that the gruesome part was over, I joined her next to the fire to help her cook the incredibly small amount of meat. She finished skewering the pieces. By my estimation, it would be less than half of what I normally ate. But it would have to do for now, since we had no other options.

"How long until it's done, do you think?"

The corners of her mouth twisted, and I knew a princeling-barb was on its way. "Never cooked a meal in your life, have you?"

"Well, you know, I normally have the servants roast my meat over the fire when I'm marooned on an island."

She cracked a smile, and I was pleased to see she no longer took me seriously. "Not that long, since it's not much meat. But it'll last us for the morning, at least. And then we can catch more."

I winced. "Poor bunnies."

"You seem to have a weak stomach for a doctor."

"You *killed* an animal right in front of me," I said. "I normally try not to kill patients."

"Have you?"

I swallowed. "I didn't get to spend much time in my residency, but...one patient died on my watch when I was interning. But he was a hundred years old and died with his whole family around him, so it wasn't like snapping the neck of an innocent bunny."

"You have to get over that," she replied. "Out here, it's kill or starve."

I nodded in agreement, but I didn't much like the concept.

We fell into an uneasy silence, watching the meat brown on the sticks in hungry anticipation. I was nearly drooling by the time she pulled the sticks off the fire. But it was a bite, gone in a matter of seconds. And I was hungrier than when we'd started.

"We'll find more," she said, tossing the used sticks into the fire. "But don't expect to be full any time soon."

"I need to lose a few pounds." I tried to force a laugh, but it came out half-hearted.

"Still." She sounded contemplative. "How *do* you suppose a rabbit and a wolf got on this island?"

"Swam?"

"I don't remember much before the crash, but I don't think there are any nearby land masses. Which means that anything that didn't fly or swim here was *brought* here."

"If someone else were here, they would've seen all the explosions," I reasoned.

"Unless they haven't been here for a long time. These islands have been disputed territory for decades. Maybe they just left livestock. Maybe that wasn't a wolf at all yesterday, but a feral dog."

"Looked awfully wolf-like to me," I grunted, remembering the sharp fangs. "What are we close to, Herin? Maybe they send ships up here every once in a while?"

"Probably too busy cowering to your father's demands," she muttered.

My head snapped around to her. "Comment?"

"Just saying that it's a bit shady that Herin promises neutrality, and yet continues to trade with Kylae as if they aren't bombing the hell out of Rave every day."

I paused. "Not *every* day."

Her eyes flashed. "Then why was I up in my plane *every day* prowling the skies for your father's planes? Why do you think we're even *at* war in the first place?"

"Oh, who the hell cares?" I said with a sigh. "I don't want to get into a political debate."

"Right, because tens of thousands of my countrymen dying every day is a political debate. *Children* dying is a political debate."

"Theo, I am not in the mood," I groaned.

"Because you're so lucky that you can be in the mood to talk about such theoretical topics," she hissed. "In case you missed it, *my people are being annihilated!*"

"Yeah, well..." I shrugged, my hunger speaking for me. I didn't want to talk politics; I just wanted a steak. "Maybe if Rave would stop being so stubborn and just come back to Kylae, they wouldn't get bombed."

THEO

My mouth fell open. In an instant, all of the goodwill I had built toward him evaporated.

"I... Are you serious? Come back? *Come back?* As if we would *ever* consider rejoining a country that's been systematically *murdering* us for half a century!"

He shrugged and sat back, looking nonchalantly towards the forest. "Is there any more food?"

My eyes narrowed. *There* was the selfish princeling I had been waiting for. Carelessly and casually dismissing the hundreds of thousands of Ravens who had died fighting for our freedom from tyranny. He was more interested in his own selfish needs than those of my people. He had been without food for a *day*, and my people sometimes went weeks on stale bread alone.

And I had *fed* the bastard. Comforted him in his moment of weakness. It was all I could do not to throw up in disgust at myself.

"If you want more food," I managed to spit out, "you'll have to get it yourself."

He turned to look at me and his eyebrows went up in confusion. "W-what was that for?"

"For killing my people," I spat. "And not caring."

"Now hold on a second," he said. "I haven't killed a single person—ever." He paused and gave me an appraising glance. "How many of *my people* have you shot down, *Captain*?"

"*Hundreds*," I snarled, pushing myself to stand. "Because you were *invading my country*."

"If Rave would just quit resisting..."

"You're unbelievable," I snapped. I had to leave this conversation before I lost my temper and beat the shit out of him. I could barely stand him as it was, but when he started spouting his Kylaen hubris...that was my limit.

"Oh, did I offend you with the truth?" he taunted.

"You offend me with your disgusting face and your stupid Kylaen arrogance."

"Arrogant, am I?" He laughed, and my blood boiled. "You're sitting here telling me I'm responsible for something I had no part in! Something that began before I was even born! In case you didn't notice, *I have no power.*"

"You think that absolves you of blame? You are the king's son —"

"And in case it wasn't glaringly obvious, the *king* isn't coming for me!"

I ignored his attempt to garner sympathy. It wasn't news to me that King Grieg was ruthless, and in my eyes, the deaths of my people were more important than the idiot princeling in front of me.

"Look, trust me, I know my father isn't in the right here," he said, standing to face me. "But at the same time, Rave's no picnic either. Sending their children to war? How can you sit there and defend something so heinous? You were conscripted at *twelve*, Theo—"

"We wouldn't have to send our children to war if Kylae would let us go!" I growled, unable to comprehend how he could defend his country after all the atrocities they'd committed.

"But you know my father will never let that happen."

"Is that how it is in Norose?" I laughed derisively. "The king makes a command and everyone just bows and says 'Yes, sire?'" I clicked my tongue against my teeth.

"Yeah, because if you disagree with him, you usually end up..." He clammed up, and the faintest of a blush appeared on his cheeks.

"End up where, princeling?" I licked my lips in delicious anticipation. I knew what he was talking about, and he knew that I knew. It was my trump card, the lovely little knife I could dig into his back.

"Mael."

SEVEN

GALIAN

Mael, the prison to the north of Norose. The mountains around our capital city were the source of a workable ore, barethium, which was mined by prisoners and processed at the work camp and used to make our planes and buildings.

My father's scientists said the smelting process was safe, and provided charts and empirical data showing that there was no danger to the prisoners. But the sheer number of deaths that occurred there every year, mostly from lung cancer and tumors, told a different story. The scientists chalked it up to pre-existing conditions, but I knew of more than one prisoner who'd begged for the death penalty instead of a stint in Mael.

She watched my expression and I suddenly hated that I had nothing to say to defend myself. There was no way to make Mael less of an atrocity than it was, and no way to separate myself from the horrors there.

"M...my mother is trying to make it safer," I stammered.

Theo's haughty laughter filled the space between us. "I'm sure the daughter of your country's wealthiest families truly cares about the plight of the lowliest criminals."

That set me off. "Don't talk about my mother like you know her."

"I know her," Theo sneered. "She's just like the rest of you. Weak, morally vacant—"

"I mean it, *stop*." I approached Theo, balling my fists. I wasn't sure I could hit her, but I was getting really close. My mother was a saint and I wouldn't have Theo insulting her.

"What are you going to do, princeling? Sentence me to a six-month visit to your death camp?"

"You forget that I'm the one who can *walk*, Captain," I spat back at her, and she retracted a little. But it was enough. "You're pretty high and mighty for someone I've saved not once, but *twice*." Her eyes narrowed. "Now I'm wondering why I even bothered. You're nothing but a disgusting Raven idiot. You're like a feral cat, hissing and spitting at the hand that feeds you. You would rather starve in the cold than—"

She punched me, right in the jaw, and my head spun. I rubbed the area, knowing it would bruise, and wondered if I had it in me to punch her right back.

She was panting, seething, and her knuckles were red. And I knew I could hit her back, but something stopped me. It wasn't some kind of chivalrous macho thing; rather, it was pity. I could destroy this girl with a flick of my wrist, but that would be like drowning that feral cat. She was halfway to death as it was.

"Well?" she growled.

I rolled my eyes and walked over to our small supplies.

"Walking away?" she called after me. "Too afraid to hit a girl?"

I ignored her taunts and retrieved the flare gun, sticking it into the waistband of my pants. I didn't know where I was going or what I was doing, but I needed to get away from her before I did something I would regret.

"You're weak, princeling!" she cried after me as I left the safety of the camp and trudged through the empty forest.

THEO

I wanted him to hit me, to get angry at me. To show me that he wasn't as uncaring as he seemed, that perhaps somewhere beneath his handsome smile and joking attitude, he was a decent person.

But sadly, everything I'd guessed about him was true. I hated how much that disappointed me. It seemed in the short amount of time we had spent together, he'd grown on me just a little. And for all his bluster, I wanted him to be better than he was. To give me some hope that Kylae and Rave could one day stop the bloody war that had raged on for two generations.

My stomach rumbled ominously. It might have been less difficult if I hadn't eaten at all. Having a small amount of food had been just enough to twist my stomach into a ravenous state. I moved to walk toward our trap, but the searing pain that shot up my leg was irrefutable. I wasn't going anywhere any time soon.

I slouched to the ground and became aware of the sounds of the forest, now so much more alive than when I'd had the princeling with his two healthy legs and ability to fight off that which would eat us. The wolf (or feral dog, didn't much matter to me what I called it) was still fresh in my mind. I'd never been that scared in my entire life, which was saying something considering the amount of danger I'd been in for most of it. But dying in a plane was quick, usually on impact. I shuddered to think about the slow, painful gory death of being eaten piece by piece.

I glanced up at the sky. It was getting dark. Soon, it would be as pitch black as the night before. The small fire in front of me was healthy, but not enough to last until morning. For a moment, my gaze darted the direction the princeling had gone. I seriously doubted he was coming back.

I scooted forward on my rear, testing out different ways to move while I attempted to gather kindling before giving up. My leg hurt too badly from the use that day. So, I tossed the small twigs into the fire and settled back into the spot I had claimed for myself.

GALIAN

I walked for a long time. I was angry that she was right about Mael and my father. Angry because there was nothing I could do about either of them. But most of all, angry that Theo blamed me for not doing anything about them.

Then, as darkness descended around me, I had other things to worry about. I was alone out there and still a little fuzzy on how to start a fire. But for the first time, I didn't want to turn around and crawl back to her. I wanted to prove to her—to myself, more—that I could survive without her.

Who's the princeling now, huh?

I gathered some sticks and brush and worked at them the way I'd seen Theo doing. After a few minutes, my hands got tired and there was no fire. I tossed the sticks down and grunted. It wasn't *that* cold; I could survive one night without heat.

I settled against a tree and wrapped my arms around myself. My thoughts drifted back to the argument, and my anger was warmth enough.

True, I was the king's son, but I didn't have any more power over him than Theo did. It was one thing to stand there and criticize, but another to actually do something about it. Was I supposed to simply waltz into that prison and announce that I wasn't leaving until they closed it down? And what of me? My father might just toss me in there with the rest of them. Or worse. We'd had a few assassinations over the past few years, and although my father had blamed them on Rave, the targets had all been his political opponents.

Considering he'd left me for dead on an island, I was smart to keep my mouth shut.

I let out a long breath, realizing how completely awful that sounded. I was afraid my own father was going to kill me for disagreeing with him. Grieg was a horrible man, cut from the same cloth as my grandfather and great-grandfather who'd started the war. Thormond had been king when Rave declared independence, and my mother told me that the castle shook with his fury when news reached him. That island was *his* and *his alone*, and those people, he'd bombed, belonged to him.

The truth of that account has long been in debate. Our public relations team had spun a good story about how the Ravens couldn't govern themselves, that they were sitting on an island full of barethium that they weren't doing anything with. They needed the guiding hand of Kylae to help them reach their full potential.

Even as a child, I'd known that was bullshit. This whole war was about resources.

Thormond's scientists were the first to discover how to make barethium usable. Up until that point, it had simply been a metal in the ground. Once they realized they could use it to make stronger buildings and stronger weapons, they'd mined it out of the Kylaen mountains until they realized the heavy human toll. The ore was deep in the rock, and required more than a bit of blasting to get to it.

When the same material was discovered in Rave, but much easier to extract, Thormond had moved processing operations to our colony. He built a few dozen giant processing plants, the pride and joy of the Kylaen empire on our colony's soil and recruited its citizens to work it. That was the final straw for the Ravens, who'd been living under our rule for some two hundred years.

They declared independence and destroyed my great-grandfather's plants. Raven statues were erected in the wreckage. Shortly thereafter, we began bombing them.

But that didn't mean *I* had anything to do with it. It was unfair of Theo to lump me in with the rest of them. I'd done what I could— gone to medical school and helped people. Her people, in fact, many of whom crowded into our cities to escape the war.

Or, I supposed, the conscription. My blood boiled harder.

Still, the refugees escaped Rave just to end up in our slums. While I was never allowed there, when you work at a hospital, eventually everyone comes to you. Many of the sick children who showed up in our emergency room had had very curable diseases at one point, but they had resisted coming to the hospital until the illness was severe. I'd always considered that simple ignorance of medical procedure, but now I wondered if there was another reason. Maybe they thought they'd be sent back to the war if they were found living there.

As I sat there, freezing my ass off on an island far away from the war, I wondered which fate was worse for them.

THEO

I found that if I rested for a while, I could walk around long enough to gather some firewood. After a few trips, the fire was now roaring and warm. However, my leg ached terribly and the gash in my other leg was starting to twinge as well. But I was still grateful the princeling was gone.

Between my trips to gather firewood, I mulled over our argument. I could not believe he'd suggested my country would be better off coming back to Kylae. Then again, the princeling seemed disconnected from it. Locked away in his mighty castle at Norose, he didn't have to wonder if he was going to die every single day. Rave couldn't go on the offensive while we had barely enough firepower to defend our shores. But if the war impacted Kylaen lives as much as it did mine, how differently would the people of Kylae feel? I wondered if they'd even been told the truth about their history, if told some watered-down version of it?

Did they know that King Thormond had broken a two-hundred-year treaty with the Rave government? Did they know that the Kylaens had barreled through our cities and forced every able-bodied man and woman to build the precursors to Mael on Raven soil? They had fed us lies about how the plants would bring prosperity to our country, but when workers started dropping like flies, we'd had enough. We'd declared our independence not because we wanted to, but because we *had* to in order to survive as a people.

Even after we'd driven the Kylaens out of the country, we were still under constant threat of destruction. Only now, my people were servants to a different master. Whether we had a king or not, we were still tethered to Kylae. Thormond wouldn't let us go, neither had his son, and neither would Grieg. There seemed no end in sight.

How could Galian come from that bloodline? As naive and misguided as he might be on political matters, he did have a good heart. He'd saved my life, twice, without a second thought. He'd chased after me, too, when I had said hurtful things to him. I had begun to believe that he genuinely cared whether I lived or died as a person, and not just as a potential prisoner of war. Now, I wasn't so sure.

I wrapped my arms tighter around myself and noticed the Kylaen uniform I still wore. When he'd first put it on me, I had been disgusted. Now I was thankful for the extra warmth because the fire was dying. I moved my legs, but the pain was too much.

"*Damn it!*" I cried, pressing my head against the tree and glanced into the darkening forest. It had been several hours, and I'd been quite sure the princeling would've been back already if he was going to. I doubted he could really survive a night on his own, but I began to worry that he might. Then he'd never come back and I'd die of exposure or become wolf-food.

As much as it killed me to admit it, I no longer had the luxury of being patriotic if I wanted to live. I had to prioritize my own survival over defending every slight against my country. Stupid or not, I needed the princeling.

GALIAN

When dawn broke, I swallowed my pride and headed back to our camp. It was a sleepless, cold night, spent wishing I was better at making a fire. The colder I became, the less angry I was with Theo. It wasn't that I thought she was right and I was wrong; it wasn't that I forgave her. But my own survival depended on her, and as the night wore on, I realized that I needed her.

Although she'd have to knock her attitude down a few pegs before I'd take another look at that leg of hers.

I spent half the night practicing what I would say, and the various ways she would argue with me, until my head hurt. I finally agreed with myself that I'd just speak from the heart and hope she saw reason.

When I approached the camp, I saw her curled into a ball on the same side of the fire where I had left her. That fire, however, was nearly gone, and I knew that she couldn't fetch more kindling without two healthy legs.

She heard me approach, and her eyes slowly lifted up to stare at me. I saw a small hint of surprise and relief in them. I swallowed the commentary on her current state and primed myself to eat crow.

Instead, we spoke at once: "What I said last night..."

We both closed our mouths, and she averted her eyes as sure as my face began to heat up in embarrassment. Silence descended between us. Seeing a healthy-sized piece of wood nearby, I picked it up and tossed it into the flames. She watched it for a moment, a relieved smile on her face as the wood caught fire and burned brighter. I sat down next to her and enjoyed the warmth.

"So what do we do now?" she asked.

"Well, I am starving, so—"

"Galian," she said with a small laugh. My heart fluttered. "That's not what I'm talking about."

The fluttering quieted as quickly as it flared. "Maybe we need to agree to...not talk about the war."

"So we'll just pretend it doesn't exist?" Thankfully, her question wasn't laced with any heat.

"While we're on the island, the only war is between us and the elements," I said, looking down at her. "And I need you on my side, Theo. And you need me on yours." With a heavy sigh, I watched the pink sky above us. "If we ever get out of here alive, we'll worry about everything else."

She seemed to be considering her odds. After an eternity, she finally answered me. "Fine, princeling. No more talk of the war."

I grinned as she took my hand, noticing how small and frail it was inside mine. She released it and looked away, the rare moment of vulnerability causing a blush to rise on her face.

She cleared her throat and looked everywhere but at me. "Maybe I can do something with your ship? I used to do work on my own. Maybe I could fix yours."

"Yeah? You're a mechanic too?" I blew air out between my lips.

"Full of surprises, aren't you, Theophilia?"

"Call me that one more time and I'll jam this stick up your dickhole."

I coughed, shifting uncomfortably. "Yes, Captain."

EIGHT

GALIAN

Theo cursed as she tinkered with my engine. She was hoping to get it to work to power the radio, although I knew it was simply something for her to do since we had already captured breakfast for the morning. My engine was never going to start again, thanks to her bullets and the impact of the crash.

It had been four days since our fight, and over a week since we'd landed on the island, by my count. We'd settled on a tepid peace that almost resembled friendship. I think we'd both grown accustomed to the meager food allotted to us. At least, the near-constant pang of hunger was down to a dull roar for me, and I felt I could function without biting her head off.

She called me over to help her off the nose. I placed her gently on the sand to make sure she had the right weight on her good leg. She grunted to me and nodded towards the edge of the forest, where the ground was less sandy and she could hobble along a little easier. I could easily pick her up and carry her, but we weren't quite there yet.

"What do you think?" I asked, motioning back to my ship.

"I think I did a damned good job of banging it up," she said, shaking her head. "I can't get the radio to work either."

"Shame I blew up your ship," I said.

She grimaced, looking at the ground. "Yeah, she was a good girl. Kept me safe in a lot of battles."

I wasn't sure about broaching the subject of her tears, but curiosity overruled caution. "Why were you so upset?"

"It's not that." Her face grew stony. "That ship was the only thing I ever called mine. I mean, she belonged to the Raven government. But she felt like mine." She shook her head. "You wouldn't understand."

"I think I do," I said. "And I'm sorry."

She poked at the sand distractedly before wiping away the design she'd made. "It doesn't matter." She glanced out onto the blue sea before us. "We need to figure out what to do next."

"Maybe we should build a boat?" I had often thought about jumping into the ocean lapping against the dull gray sand just to get myself clean. But I was already dealing with a permanent chill, so I was sure jumping into the frigid Madion Sea probably wasn't the smartest idea.

"It's possible," she nodded, looking out into the gray water. "The seas are choppy right now, but if we can build a big enough boat to withstand the waves, and get enough food to last us for the days—or weeks..." She paused, thinking more. "We'd need a compass. There's a lot of ocean to cover."

"So that's a no, then." I sighed, looking back at the wooded area behind us. "You know, we haven't really seen all that's here on the island."

"We've been a little busy trying to survive." She followed my gaze to the forest behind us and then gave me an appraising look. "I don't think that's the best idea."

"Why not? What if there's something out there that could help us? You said yourself that those wolves and all the rabbits we've found aren't native to this island. So maybe we can find some remnants of what brought them here."

"And what about food?" she asked. "We need to make sure we have dinner before we start going on leisurely walks."

"If I could find us something, maybe we won't have to worry about food."

She didn't seem to believe I'd find anything, but she acquiesced. "At the first sign of sunset, come back. And if you run into any more of those dogs, don't engage."

"Yes, ma'am," I said with a salute. She'd sounded so captain-like that I couldn't help teasing her a little.

A small smile was my reward. "Leave me over near the traps," she said, wrapping her arm around my shoulder as I helped her up. "That way at least one of us will have dinner."

THEO

The princeling was gone before I even knew it, and I could hardly blame him. I think we were both looking for some good news.

Free to do as I pleased, I kept an eye on the rudimentary trap to my left while I attempted to make a better one. One rabbit a day wasn't enough to sustain us, so I attempted to fashion a cage to capture more at a time. Using the knife, I stripped some twigs down to a pliable width and wrapped them around thicker branches to connect them. It took me a few tries, but the joint held, and I managed to repeat it.

As I worked, my mind wandered to the princeling and the curiosity of this island. I had no idea if Galian would find anything out there, and part of me was glad that he'd gone. He'd been hovering over me like a useless hawk for two days and his attentiveness was getting on my nerves again. He was trying, and so I kept my tongue instead of barking at him.

Still, if I didn't have dinner when he returned, then we would go a night without. And I wasn't very much looking forward to that.

Yet again, I found myself leading the troops, being responsible. Being the strong one. It was exhausting. But I didn't even have time to feel sorry for myself. It was up to me to ensure our survival.

I looked at the makeshift cage and smiled. It would definitely trap a rabbit, but the question was how to keep him in there. I put down the cage and considered my options. It wasn't long before my mind wandered again.

Had someone already taken my mattress, the way I'd casually taken others' when they didn't return? Had Lanis already given up hope? Had a new captain already been promoted, taking over however many of my young pilots were left at the Vinolas base from Kylae's last invasion?

I smiled to myself. I thought I'd be a captain for maybe a year or two before Lanis managed to swing me an assignment with the armed forces headquarters in the capital city of Veres. There I could have been promoted to Major, maybe even Lieutenant Colonel. And never have to risk my life in battle again.

I'd given all that up to try to kill the princeling. That was what

I got for letting my ego get in the way. Fat load of good it had done me. Stuck on an island with the very man I tried to kill. Trying to make a cage to feed us both.

And yet, as much as I missed the availability of a warm bed and a roof over my head, I wasn't all that upset to be there. I was no longer on edge, waiting for the siren's wail that would signal an impending battle. There was still the danger of death, but I felt like it was more in my hands. As long as Galian and I stuck together, our survival chances greatly increased.

I picked up the cage again, trying to figure out the problem. But to my horror, it disintegrated in my hands, nothing but a pile of sticks. I blew air out in frustration. Perhaps the princeling was having better luck.

GALIAN

As I crept through the lush green forest, I forgot that I was marooned there and started to enjoy the fresh air and the movement. Walking briskly had warmed my cheeks and my body, I even halfway forgot that I was starving.

I was, however, not a complete idiot. I stopped every other tree to carve a long line in the bark, a marker of where I'd been so I could find my way back to camp.

I wasn't in any hurry to return though. It still felt like I was walking on eggshells around Theo—the same sort of feeling I had around my father. One wrong move, and it was disapproval and disappointment or worse.

But as I pushed aside branches and trudged through the empty forest, I was free to do whatever I wanted. I could take a left or a right or keep marching straight ahead. There wasn't much difference between one way or another, but the freedom to choose my destiny was exciting.

I stopped in the middle of underbrush and looked around, listening to the silence. I let my eyes drift along the thick trunks, the branches and the leaves, and the trees that had died and fallen over, and I found myself thinking that those stupid Kylaen tabloid photographers could have found any number of places to hide and take photos of me if they'd been there.

Although I could only imagine what I looked like, with the spotty beard growing on my face, and my hair sticking up at odd angles from the dirt and the grime of the island. My shirt was now five shades darker than when I'd left Kylae, my pants torn and singed in several places.

I could see the magazine cover now: "Prince Turned Wild Man."

I snorted as I carved another mark into the tree. They may not have even recognized me at this point. I rubbed my hand along my face, the hair annoyingly scratchy already. I'd tried to grow a beard when I was eighteen, but shaved it after a day of merciless shit from my two brothers. From the feel of my face, I could tell that I was no better at growing facial hair at twenty-five than I'd been at eighteen.

I paused as I considered Rhys and my mother, and what they must be going through to have lost a second brother and son. The ache in my chest was too much, so I soldiered onto different thoughts.

The island was bigger than I'd thought, and what seemed like a few hours later, I was still walking through nothing but forest. My stomach ached from hunger, and I began to question the intelligence of leaving. I had seen some different birds, and one or two rabbits, but I wasn't as adept at catching and killing as Theo.

I stopped in the middle of the path, realizing that I was walking up an incline. I hurried up the hill, standing on the edge.

The area was clear of trees, with overgrown brush tumbling over a gravel pathway. My eyes were drawn across the flat land to a structure in the center of the clearing. It was rusted, covered in brush. But there was no mistaking what I saw.

THEO

It was getting dark and I was now getting worried.

I poked at the fire, willing the light to glow brighter to lead the princeling back. My concern was only partially selfish, as I'd grown a little protective of His Royal Pain In My Ass.

I poked the fire again and stared at the darkening woods.

I began to second guess allowing him to leave, as if I had any say over his decision-making. But perhaps if I had gone with him, I might have been able to prevent him from making a boneheaded decision. Or from getting hurt. Or any number of outcomes my overactive imagination was now considering.

Then again, I thought, nibbling on rabbit meat still hot from the fire, I wouldn't have dinner if I'd gone strolling around the island with him.

There was no way he was going to find anything. He was wasting his time, and I needed him to help around camp.

His share of the meal was hanging on two sticks in the ground. I was still hungry, and I could rightfully eat his half of the food. After all, it was nearly pitch black out. And I thought he might already be dead.

I looked at the dark sky. I hoped he wasn't dead.

I heard movement in the dark brush, and my fingers tightened around the flare gun never more than a few inches from my hand.

"Galian?" I called into the darkness.

When no one answered, my heart raced, and I picked up the flare gun.

"Hello?" I tried again. "Galian? Is that you?"

More rustling, but this time from another direction. I shook my head to clear it, hoping that my mind was just playing tricks on me. Or it was the wind.

I lifted the gun—

"*Theo!*"

I screamed, dropping the gun before I fired it into Galian's chest. He stopped short, giving me a strange look as I covered my chest to keep my heart from beating out of it.

"Theo, I found—"

"You *idiot!*" I screamed. "*Do you even know how worried I was about you?*"

"I— You were worried?" he said with a small grin.

I pushed myself to my feet, storming over to him as angrily as I could with my stupid limp.

"Galian, I can't do much of anything without you, so please, if you're going to give me a heart attack, *don't!*"

"Sorry, but—"

"Where have you been?" I continued, ignoring him completely. "I told you to be back *before* it got dark? What if you hadn't been able to find your way back? What if you'd been injured?"

"Theo, I—"

"Galian, I know you've never had to worry about your own survival—"

"Hey!"

"But please try to have a little sympathy—"

"Theo!" he barked loudly enough to get my attention. "I found a building."

NINE

THEO

"See? I told you!"

I'd been ninety percent sure the princeling was hallucinating from hunger when he came barreling into the camp, talking about some "building" he'd found. But he'd insisted I come with him when day broke, even going as far as to carry me the whole way. His innocent excitement was a little endearing, and I'd figured it would be better to let him get it out of his system than to fight him on it.

But I'd never actually expected to see a building on this island. It was definitely military, but from which country, I wasn't sure. Judging by the overgrown vines and rusted doors, I knew it didn't matter. This place was abandoned and had been for a number of years.

"I *told* you there was a building here!" Galian repeated for the fiftieth time, walking up to the doors with a satisfied look on his face.

"Do you have a key?" I asked, looking at the thick iron front doors. His face fell, and I felt a bit guilty. "Maybe it's rusted enough that we don't need one."

He nodded and ran his hands along the door. "I didn't get a

chance to really look yesterday, but..." His fingers slipped into the cracks, and he pulled at it valiantly and pointlessly.

"Maybe there's a back entrance," I offered, hobbling over to the outer wall and peering around the corner.

"Right, because an impenetrable base would have a backdoor," Galian grunted, still pulling at the iron doors.

I glanced up at the roof, which was a particular shape, as if something large had been on top of it at one time. A grin spread across my face.

"It's not a base, it's a radar station."

Galian's voice floated from the front, laced with exertion. "And why does that make you happy?"

"Nobody reinforces a radar station," I said, using the wall to brace me. I turned a corner to the back and saw a small, less difficult-to-enter back door.

"Well, shit," Galian said, peering over my shoulder. He walked up to the flimsy door and jiggled the handle. With a grunt, he lifted his foot and slammed it into the metal, causing the door to fall off the hinges and a foul curse of pain to emanate from the princeling. Dust fell from the door frame, covering him in a new curtain of grime.

Once my eyes adjusted to the darkness, I noticed a sink, counters, and cabinets lining the walls, and small tables in the center of the room—a mess hall. Finding such a modern room on this overgrown, remote island was surreal.

"Theo, look over here." Galian had moved to the countertops, brushing dust off a dark wall.

I inched closer so I could make out the symbol better. The paint was peeling and faded, but there was no mistaking it.

"Kylaen...I think?" It resembled the lion on Galian's uniform, but it was slightly different.

"Kylaen kings change the crest when they come into power," Galian said. "This one was definitely my grand...or wait, it might have been my great-grandfather Thormand's. But it's definitely not my father's."

"So what does that mean?" I said, looking around. "This radar station hasn't been used since before the start of the war?"

Galian frowned and flipped a switch on the wall. "No electricity, either."

"But it's a shelter?" I offered. "Maybe there's supplies."

"I'm going to go check it out some more," he said, more to himself than to me. Before I could stop him, he disappeared into the darkness. I heard him banging into things every few minutes, followed by a filthy curse. Soon he was too far away for me to hear, so I used the small bit of light from the open door to explore the room.

I checked all the cabinets for any food that might still be edible half a century later and found them all barren. A couple of drawers had some left-behind serving spoons and small knives, but nothing helpful.

As I leaned against the countertop, I spotted the sink in the corner. Slowly, I twisted the knob on the faucet and held my breath. I heard air moving then black liquid sputtered out of the tap. After a few minutes, the water ran as clear as crystal.

Unabashedly, I stuck my mouth under the running water and drank until my stomach was full. I hadn't realized how thirsty I was until just this moment—making drinkable water from seawater was a tiring business. I slid to the ground, a happy smile on my face. We might not have been as screwed as I'd thought. This place was shelter from the elements, relatively warm, and had fresh running water.

It must have been sent by God. That was the only explanation that made sense to me.

GALIAN

All my excitement about this place evaporated when I saw the Kylaen crest on the wall. Not that I'd really paid attention in the military history class—Dig and Rhys were too busy making the after-school lesson a living nightmare for me. But I knew these islands weren't part of our country's land and never had been.

So what was my great-grandfather's crest doing on a wall? For that matter, what the hell was this place doing there? And what did a Kylaen base mean for my chances of getting home?

For the moment, I was focused on other things. The laceration on Theo's leg had grown a little red and warm to the touch when I last checked it, so I was hoping to find a medical kit there to clean it before it got worse. The search would have gone a bit faster had there been working light fixtures, but the dim light filtering in from the high windows was enough so I could see dark shapes.

Eventually, I banged and bounced my way into a supply closet that was full of boxes. And to my ultimate surprise, they contained medical supplies.

"Well that's...convenient," I said, pulling down a box of syringes and needles.

In fact, most of the equipment in there was for blood testing—odd for a radar station. I did manage to find a box of gloves, some gauze, and rubbing alcohol that would prove useful for cleaning the wound.

She was snoozing lightly against the mess hall cabinets when I returned, and I almost hated to wake her.

"What'd you find?" she asked with an uncharacteristically cute yawn.

I opened the rubbing alcohol and smelled it, deciding it was still good enough to use.

"Going out for a drink?" Theo asked, walking over to me.

"Hardly," I said. "Hop up, I want to clean your leg."

"We find shelter and your first thought is my leg?" She sounded surprised, maybe a little flattered. Or maybe my mind was playing tricks on me.

I tried to play it off. "You're my patient until you're fully healed."

She unzipped the jumpsuit and climbed up on the table as I prepped the gauze and the other supplies. It was damned near impossible to see as I removed the old, bloody wrapping on her leg. The wound was healing, albeit slowly, but I would still feel better if I cleaned it.

"Theo, this is going to hurt a little," I said, picking up the alcohol.

"I have come to expect that from you." She hissed when I touched the wet gauze to her open wound, but said nothing else.

"Boy, this is going to scar something awful, I'm sorry," I said, hoping to distract her as I cleaned. "I wish I'd had more sutures in the bag to sew it tighter."

"Scar is better than being dead," she replied. "I've been wondering...where *did* that bag come from?"

"I haven't told you about Maitland yet?" I said, surprised that it had taken me this long to broach the subject.

"Don't..." She inhaled loudly as I cleaned deep into the wound. "...recall."

"Dr. Maitland is the royal physician at the hospital. He's the one who inspired me to go into medicine."

"Mm-hmm?"

"He gave me that medical supply bag. And taught me that a life is important, no matter what country it comes from."

She opened her mouth to retort, but then closed it. I had a good idea what she was going to say, and I appreciated her holding her comment. Instead, she asked, "Why did he give you a bag of medical supplies to raid a country?"

I smiled. "I doubt Dr. Maitland expected I'd actually use it. I think it was supposed to be more symbolic."

She turned to look back at me. "For what?"

"He wanted me to remember that I could make my own decisions," I said, remembering our last conversation and wondering if he had given up hope that I'd come back alive. "That I'm not my father's man."

"Dangerous words," she said, wincing as I tucked the end of the gauze into place. "But good ones."

"I still got into that plane," I said with a laugh. "Maybe I should have taken his advice after all..."

"How does it feel?" I asked.

"Hurts."

"Better or worse than it did?"

She let out a breath. "Worse. But...better."

I picked up a thick roll of gauze and wrapped it tightly. "Hopefully I can find another roll of this stuff so it won't get infected.

How does your other leg feel?" I asked, picking up her left foot to check on the break in her lower leg. It was a garish purple now, and I wished I could at least take a scan of it to check on the severity of the injury.

"Ow." She winced as I gently turned it to the left.

"Sorry." I set her leg down and glanced around the kitchen. "Let me see what I can do to get a better brace for you."

"Galian." Something about the way my name rolled off her tongue drew my attention. "I think my leg will be fine. What else did you find in here? Any chance there's electricity?"

I ducked into one of the cabinets and ran my hands along the dusty shelves, coming up empty. "There are lights here, so they obviously had to have turned on somehow."

"Or maybe they found a way to make it self-sufficient."

"I'd say the latter," I said, considering the distance and the resources required to lay electrical wire from Kylae as I peered in another cabinet. "This place is too far from anything."

"There's a good chance it's water powered, since I didn't see any wind generators or solar panels," she said, pushing herself off the table. "Interested in looking for a hydroelectric generator?"

"Oh, I thought you'd never ask..."

THEO

We left the small kitchen, Galian leading the way, and me bracing myself on his arm as I hobbled behind him. He showed me the

113 | S. USHER EVANS

open closet where he said he'd found the gauze and alcohol to clean my wounds. We checked a few more boxes to see if there was anything else, but it was more of the same.

"If I wanted to check your blood cholesterol levels, I'd be all set," Galian said, picking up another syringe from a box. "But you'd have to fast first, of course."

I snorted at his joke and rubbed my empty stomach. We should have probably looked for food, but I was a little more excited about our new sanctuary.

The station was a series of long hallways lined with locked doors. Galian insisted on stopping at each room, using his body weight and shoulder to break the lock on the door. We found a set that appeared to be either barracks or prison cells. My guess was the latter, considering there was only one bed in each room and it was devoid of anything else...but why would there be prison cells in a radar station?

The puzzle grew more interesting when we found another set of rooms also empty except for a single bed—though these beds were metal with leather restraints on them.

"This is an operating room," Galian announced, sounding as perplexed as I was.

"What's an operating room doing here?" I asked, running my hands over the restraints. They looked very well-used, although their age was starting to show.

"What is *any* of this doing here?" Galian muttered to himself as we continued on.

In the last hallway, we finally found something promising. A red door with *No Entry—Authorized Personnel Only* on it. It took Galian a few tries, but the door finally gave way to a pitch black staircase.

"Are you going down there?" I asked, peering down the darkness.

"Yeah, piece of cake," Galian said, grasping at the wall until he found the railing. "You stay here. I don't want you breaking something else."

"Speak for yourself," I said as he stumbled down a step.

I caught a glare from him before he disappeared. I eased down on the top stair, my thigh wound stinging. I smiled as I touched the bandage under the jumpsuit. My first concern was how well this place boded for our survival—there was water, shelter, warmth, possibly food if we could find something unexpired. But Galian's worry was my leg. He'd said it was because I was his patient, but there was something else there, too. Or perhaps I'd just never been cared for in my entire life, and this was how it felt to have someone worry if I lived or died.

Either way, I liked it very much.

"Theo! I found something!"

"Really?" I popped my head up. "Do you need me to come down there?"

"Stay...up there..." He grunted, as if pushing something.

I heard rushing water, and immediately my heart began to quicken. "Galian?" I called.

"I'm okay," he replied. "Just give it a sec."

Machines and gears that hadn't moved in over half a century groaned and squeaked as they churned forward by the water.

The staircase shook as he ascended to join me at the top. Above us, a light flickered to life, bathing us in a grimy, dingy glow.

I looked over at Galian and shared a smile with him.

"You were right," he said. "Hydroelectric generator. How'd you know?"

I shrugged. "Lucky guess."

"This whole place is a lucky guess," Galian said, leaning back.

With the basement lights on, I could now see the small water wheel at the bottom and the latch Galian had opened to let in the sea water. I was mesmerized by the water pushing the wheel forward, which squeaked pleasantly every few turns.

"You look more relaxed than I've ever seen you," Galian observed.

"Shelter will do that to me, I suppose," I said with a laugh. "And working lights."

"Well, I saw something that will make you even *happier* than shelter."

"Food?"

He faltered a little. "Okay, not that happy. But the bathrooms are right over there."

GALIAN

I stood under the bone-chilling cold water spraying out of the shower head and couldn't have been happier. I'd probably been in there for much longer than was healthy, especially considering the temperature, but I didn't care. I had long since used up the remnants of the harsh lye soap caked onto the soap holder and now I was just standing under the water, enjoying the feeling of being clean.

"Did you drown in there, princeling?" Theo called from the other side of the wall.

"I hear the water running on your side, too!" I barked back at her.

Suddenly, I began to imagine the cold water dripping down her naked body, puckering her skin.

I coughed, more to quell the thoughts in my own head. It was a good thing the water was cold. I hadn't thought about Theo in that way in some time, not when we were so busy trying to survive. But even now that things were a little easier, I was pretty sure there was no way she'd ever consent to sleeping with me. All my explicit thoughts served to do was give me an erection and nothing to do with it.

"I'm stepping out," she said.

I closed my eyes and tried not to think of her naked again. "Good."

"I didn't want to offend your delicate princeling sensibilities." There was a note of playfulness in her voice I hadn't heard before. Now I *really* couldn't stop thinking about her naked.

"Oh? You'll recall I'm a doctor," I said, more for myself than for her. "Did you get your bandage wet?"

"No, Dr. Princeling, you only told me four times not to," she said from the common area between the showers. I told myself not to look, trying to remind myself that she was technically my patient and I wasn't supposed to be wondering what she looked like naked.

But my fingers pulled open the shower curtain and I caught a glimpse of her. I already knew she was too thin in the ribcage, I knew the shape of her thighs. But now I was looking at the whole woman, the curve of her breasts, the way her long, wet hair clung to her back as she bent over to dry herself off.

Before she noticed me watching her, I tore my eyes away, stepping into the cold water again that was suddenly much more necessary.

When I emerged, Theo was gone, as was one of the sets of old Kylaen uniforms I had found in the supply closet. It was nice to slide on something that wasn't the disgusting white shirt and khakis I had been wearing since landing there. Even if it did smell like moldy cotton.

I followed the hallway from the showers to the dormitories we'd found. Eight bunks of two beds each were stacked neatly on the walls. Theo was curled up in the one furthest away from me, her wet hair dangling over the edge of the bed.

I sat down in a bunk directly opposite from her, finding it silly to sleep far away when we were the only two people there.

"It's almost like I'm back home," she said wistfully.

"This is home?"

"I suppose the Kylaen military housing is a bit more private?"

I blushed. "I...uh...wouldn't know."

"Ah," she said, rolling onto her belly. "So the princeling never had to bunk with his troops?"

"No," I said with a small shake of my head. "Too dangerous for me to be out of the castle."

"Was that their estimation or yours?"

I saw the playful smile on her face. "What do you want me to say? The 'princeling' wanted to sleep in his own bed."

She pressed down on the mattress as if testing it. "This one actually is softer than the ones we have back in Rave. I consider myself an expert in mattresses."

"Oh?" It was now hard to not think about her naked in the shower.

She caught my meaning and blushed. "I mean, I used to steal mattresses from people when they...when they didn't come back.

Trying to find the most comfortable one."

"Do you think someone's swiped your mattress yet?"

"Probably before the sun went down on the first day." Her face tightened. "They aren't going to waste resources to look for me. I'm not...I'm not important."

"I've been wondering," I said, leaning back onto the highly uncomfortable mattress. "You didn't seem surprised to see me."

"Hm?"

"After you crashed, you didn't seem surprised to see me on the island with you."

"I knew who I'd shot down."

"How?"

"You made the unfortunate mistake of alerting us to your participation in the air raid by speaking to your brother."

My cheeks reddened. I'd forgotten about my selfish and irresponsible conversation with Rhys. Possibly the last I'd ever have with him.

"Sorry, by the way," she whispered. "For shooting you down. For getting us stuck here."

I cocked my head to the side. "I thought you were just following orders."

She snorted and looked at the wool coverlet on the bed. "I didn't have an order to go after you. I knew it was you and, I thought if I shot you down, I'd get promoted out of...battle."

"I might have been pissed off a few days ago," I said, looking around us at the bunker. "But now I know what true survival is like. You take what you can get. I would've killed me if it meant I could get off this island."

She glanced up at me again then back down without saying

anything.

I laughed and laid down in the bed, turning my head to look at her. "Did you consider killing me?"

"Yes," she said without hesitation. "But...it seemed rather ungrateful considering you'd just saved my life. And it's easier to shoot down some faceless evil Kylaen in the sky than the person sitting across from you, breathing, eating, talking."

"But you've killed people before."

"I didn't have a choice," she whispered, looking at the ceiling. "I try not to think about all of the people I've..." She swallowed. "But when someone's shooting at you, there's only one way to get them to stop."

I considered the seven years she'd spent in the Raven military. My one flight was enough to convince me that I never wanted to do it again. My admiration for her resolve grew.

"Did you ever get scared?" I asked.

"Every time I got in my plane," she said with a sad smile. "But I realized early on that I don't have the luxury of being scared. Not here. Not in the air. Not until my plane was back in the hangar."

"Then what?"

"Then I cried myself to sleep."

I could see the toll so many years of keeping it together had taken on her. I wished for a tenth of her strength, but at the same time, I was grateful I didn't have to have it.

"Look at the bright side," I said, cocking my head. "You kind of did get your freedom by shooting me down. You are free to do whatever you want now."

"I like that about you, princeling." She yawned, curling up under the covers again. "You always look at the positive."

I turned my head to comment, but she was asleep with a sweet, content smile on her face. So, after turning off the lights, I settled back onto the uncomfortable mattress, pulling the scratchy wool blanket over me, enjoying the first bit of good luck I'd had since I landed on this stupid island.

Or, I thought, looking over at Theo, the second.

TEN

THEO

When the ache in my leg woke me the next morning, I momentarily forgot where I was. The familiar lumpy feeling of a mattress lulled me into thinking I was back in Rave. But no, I was still on the island, the princeling sleeping soundly on the next bed over.

I decided that being there was no longer terrible. I was hungry, of course, but I was warm and I'd had a good night's sleep, undisturbed by worry about waking up to fangs in my face. Most of all, the princeling had grown on me and it warmed me to see his sleeping face. He was easy to talk to—and not because he was my only conversation partner. And, if I were being completely honest, I'd caught a glimpse of his naked body before he'd jumped into the shower, and it had left me thinking about crawling into bed with him.

I smiled to myself. My lieutenants would've thrown themselves at him on the first night. If we were ever rescued, I could just imagine the media storm—

My amused thoughts ended as quickly as they'd begun. It made no sense for me to become attached to the princeling. Us being an "us" would never work, and even entering that territory was asking for heartache.

In the next bed over, Galian stirred and opened one eye. "Morning."

"Morning," I said, curling under the covers.

"Do you think there's anything to eat in this place?" he asked with a huge yawn.

I smiled. At least he was starting to prioritize the right things. "Doubtful. If they left anything behind, I'm sure it's expired by now. I'd rather not die of food poisoning."

He grimaced and rolled over. "So we have still to go hunt for breakfast still?"

I laughed and kicked off the covers, sitting up and stretching. "You'd think you'd be used to it by now."

"Hope springs eternal, Theo..."

This side of the island was teeming with rabbits. Once I had fashioned a trap, we caught four of them in one fell swoop. I'd almost forgotten what it was like to be full.

After our meal, we set to exploring the radar station now that we had light inside. When the Kylaens abandoned this place, they'd taken everything with them, save the supply closet. We found more operating rooms and jail cells, and I looked through every cabinet in the mess hall, unearthing exactly three cans of vegetables that had expired forty years before.

"Theo, look in here," Galian called from down the hall. I followed the sound of his voice into a room filled with screens and old computers. Galian stood in the center, a nearly maniacal smile on his face.

"What's this?" I asked.

"Looks like it's the control center," he said, turning to press the buttons on the machines. To my surprise, they hummed to life.

"Interesting."

"Theo, these might still be hooked into Kylae," Galian said, a little breathlessly.

I stopped for a moment, my face falling along with my hopes.

"If we can get these to work, maybe we can get a message out to someone," Galian said. "These things are older than dirt, but maybe there's a way you can tap into the Kylaen airwaves and—"

He stopped when he saw the look on my face. I knew I could probably fashion a half-assed signaling system, if Galian could tell me what frequency Kylae operated on.

But I wasn't sure I wanted to.

"What?" he asked.

"If we do call for help, let me be far away from here," I said, knowing I was resigning myself to one fate if I were left there. But if I went, I'd be resigning myself to another. In the optimism and company of Galian, I'd let myself forget that I was going to die soon.

"Theo..." He stood up. "Don't say that."

I cocked my head at him. "Galian, I'm serious. There is no way going to Kylae ends well for me."

He grabbed my hands and held them together. "You can't be serious. To stay here?"

"I'm dead either way," I whispered. At least if I remained on the island, I'd have a chance of staying alive a few extra...weeks.

"You remember what I promised you?" He tightened his grip. "When we first landed on this island, I told you I wasn't going to let you die, remember?"

"Galian—"

"No," he insisted. "I am a lot of things, but when I say something, I *mean* it. You're coming with me off this island."

A fresh wave of heat rose in my face from the way he held my hands and the intense look on his face.

"First, let me see if I can get it to work," I said, freeing my hands. "Then we'll talk about what happens next."

GALIAN

I tried not to hover over Theo as she tinkered with the electrical wires, now splayed around her. But it was damned hard not to.

If this place was Kylaen, at one point it had been connected to our military networks. If we could just get one computer working again, it might be enough to alert someone. The thought was so exciting I could barely sit still.

I didn't care what Theo said, I wasn't going to leave her there. It was suicide, and she knew it. I wouldn't be able to live with myself knowing she was back there starving while I was back in my bed.

Then again—I tossed her another look—I wondered if she'd ever consider sharing that bed with me.

She caught me staring at her so I stood to leave her be. If I pissed her off, she wouldn't help me. A small part of me wondered if she was just pretending to fix the computers, but that wasn't the Theo I knew.

I strolled down the halls to burn off my nervous energy. This place was still a mystery to me, but I no longer cared. I could go back to not caring about things like this. I could go back to filling my head with obscure diseases and intubation techniques. I wasn't sure what I'd do with Theo when I got there, but I'd figure it out. Maybe she could dye her hair blonde and just say she was really, really tanned.

I blanched, thinking of Theo as a blonde.

I stopped in front of an office we'd opened but not explored earlier in the day. It was small, with a built-in desk, and shelves and cabinets lining the walls. I sat in the small chair and thumbed through some of the paperwork, wondering if Theo had gotten the computer to work yet.

"Don't piss her off," I whispered to myself.

I forced myself to read the binder in front of me, which turned out to be a medical file.

"So those were operating rooms," I said, still puzzling over why my great-grandfather would see fit to place a medical facility on a deserted island, and disguise it as a radar station. None of this made sense to me at all.

I put on my Doctor Helmuth hat—since I was going back to the hospital and all, I supposed it would be good to practice again—and read through the patient file. Except, the more I looked at it, the less it seemed like a patient file. It was about a person, sure, but it seemed unnervingly clinical. The patient name was a number, the notes were specific to test results, not a word on how the patient felt.

I flipped back to the front of the binder, looking for more information. Buried deep within the paragraphs of introductory tests, my eyes couldn't believe what they read.

"During the process of smelting Kylaen weapons from raw barethium, a small amount of airborne barethium is released. Barethium is

a known toxin to the human body. In large quantities, it causes aggressive malignant tumors, renal and liver failure, and, if ingested, is almost always fatal.

I sat back, mouth open. Not even a year before, the Kylaen scientists had shown my mother research proving the exact opposite.

What remains to be seen is how much inhaled barethium will cause the severe reactions seen in ingested amounts. Initial tests on rabbits and mice indicate that a human could withstand two hundred times the level of inhaled barethium before side effects begin to occur. This facility has begun a trial of inhaled barethium on Raven slaves—"

I slammed the binder shut, my heart and stomach in my mouth.

THEO

Silence was golden as I worked on the computers. Even though it was sixty years old, the circuitry was scarily similar to what we had in Rave. I twisted two wires together while considering how our technological advancement was stymied, whereas Kylae continued to move forward.

"Bastards," I muttered to myself.

I sat up and pressed a button on the computer and cursed when the machine did nothing. Lying back down, I unhooked the two wires and tried a different set. My fingers singed as the active currents touched each other and the computer hummed to life. Our lifeline back to civilization was working.

Galian was going to go home, back to his family, his castle, his full meals. For him, I was happy that I could save his life for once and relieved to clear the ledger between us. I was surprised at how sad I became knowing he'd soon be out of my life. We had only spent a short time together, but I had grown more attached to him than I'd thought.

I heard his footfalls down the hall and I crawled out from under the circuitry.

"Well, it's working. Do you happen to know the frequency for —" I stopped when I saw his ashen face and knew something was very wrong. "What is it?"

He gripped a binder like it held some closely guarded secret. "I found something you need to see."

"What is it?"

He hesitated for a second, looking down at the binder. "Please don't...don't think any less of me."

I furrowed my brow. "Why would anything of yours be in here?"

"Not me, but..." He sighed heavily and thrust the binder at me. "Just...please remember that..."

I almost didn't want to look inside. With trembling hands, I opened the binder. The first page was refreshingly devoid of anything horrifying; it was simply a cover page. A report of a test that had been conducted in the radar station. I flipped the pages, seeing text and numbers and lots of things that didn't make sense.

Then I saw the first photo.

"Oh my God..."

It was a person—a Raven, to be exact. But I could only tell because of the label on the photo. Strapped to one of those operating tables, the body was so disfigured and discolored that I couldn't even tell it was human anymore. The mouth was open at an odd angle, as if the person had screamed themselves to death. Purple splotches covered the arms, evidence that the patient had tried to free himself from the restraints. Giant tumors stuck out from the shoulder, the knee, the stomach.

"W-what is this?" I whispered to Galian, who looked about as sick as I felt.

"I think...I think this was a secret testing laboratory," he replied. "There are other binders of experiments with animals. That's where all the rabbits came from."

"What were they testing?" I asked. "What could they possibly have been testing that would have warranted this kind of...horrifying..."

"They wanted to test the effects of barethium on humans," he whispered.

"Barethium?" The name sounded familiar, but I couldn't place it.

"It's the...it's..." He couldn't look at me, and that made me even sicker. "Mael."

"Mael?" I said, looking down at the binder again.

"Barethium is the ore that they're mining out of the mountains, the same ore that's found in Rave," he said quietly. "This lab was to test how much a human could take before it was fatal."

"Ravens. They were testing on Ravens," I whispered, covering my mouth.

He plopped down in a chair across from me. "When my mother went to the Kylaen royal scientists to try and prove Mael was well, killing people, they told her they'd done tests and showed her proof that it was safe."

I glanced up at him. "You can't be serious. All of the people who die there every year?"

"Pre-existing conditions," he replied hollowly. "That's what they say. But this proves that they know. They've *known!* They knew before they built the first plant in Rave. They knew before... they knew before they even tested on humans. And they did it anyway."

I closed my eyes. "The wolves? Did they test on them, too?"

He shook his head. "I think...they were guard dogs. There are photos and..."

I couldn't think of it anymore; I couldn't stand to be in this place. The knowledge of the atrocities committed there was suffocating. The ghosts of my ancestors pressed in on me, as if the very mention of their suffering had drawn them.

"Theo, where are you going?" Galian called after me.

"Back to the camp. I'm not spending another *minute* in this place." I knew it would take me all day to get there, but I didn't care. I barreled through the kitchen, ignoring the visions of Kylaen doctors and guards eating their leisurely lunches while torturing and killing human beings in rooms down the hall.

"Stop." Galian grabbed my arm and spun me around. "I know this is shocking and sickening. Trust me, I'm just as disgusted as you are."

"But what?"

"This all happened years ago," Galian said and my anger flared.

"So we should just let it go?" I growled.

"Not let it go, but we need to—"

"What about the fact that your people are *still exploiting mine!*"

"Theo, now's not the time to get into all that—"

"And when is a good time, *Your Highness,*" I spat the phrase at him. "When all the Ravens are dead? When you've got your hundred square miles of country back?"

"How about after we call for help?" he barked at me. "Let's get off this island and then we'll deal with all of the shit that happened here. We'll raze this entire place to the ground!"

"*Look around you*!" I screamed. "I'm *Raven*! This place is how your people see me—nothing but an animal to experiment on! Do you think they'll let me live a second in your country? Are you that stupid to think that just because you snap your fingers, everyone will forget what I am?"

Galian watched me helplessly. Even though I was nauseated, furious, disgusted, and all manner of other feelings I couldn't name, I still felt pity for him. He was different than the rest of his family, the rest of his country, even. But in this case, his blinding optimism was to his detriment.

"I'm sorry, Theo," he said. "I truly... I wish..."

"The radio is on," I said. "If you can find the Kylaen frequency, you can call for help. I'll be long gone."

He didn't argue with me. Prince Galian Helmuth of Kylae had finally realized just how depraved his country really was. And that was victory enough for me.

GALIAN

I didn't go after her. I should have, but I didn't. What was there for me to say to her to make this place right? What could I have done to erase all this horror sanctioned by my own ancestor?

There was no universe in which these atrocities would ever be forgiven. I could save a thousand lives, and it wouldn't make up for the ones taken there. Even more, we continued to subject prisoners to the deadly fumes at Mael, knowing the consequences—and lied about it to our own people.

I glanced at the door, again wishing I could follow Theo. But I didn't feel worthy of her presence.

There was something wrong with getting to leave this island after what I'd just discovered. I deserved to suffer for the sins of my forefathers. Theo should've been the one who went home.

I wasn't sure how long I sat in front of the radio, tapping my fingers on the dashboard, thinking, before I tried to use it. Rhys was a radio operator in the Kylaen military, but I'd never spent any time learning, so I had no idea what to do.

There were two buttons in front of me, green and black, and a dial that adjusted the frequency. I pressed the black one and heard static echo through the speakers on the dashboard. Pressing the green one stopped the static, but alighted a small red light on the microphone.

"Hello?"

No answer.

I spun the frequency dial slowly, listening for chatter. I did two passes through all the frequencies and heard none.

"Shit."

Trying again, I pressed the green button and spoke into the microphone, waiting a half second before moving to the next one. When that didn't work, I sat back and lazily moved the dial, now considering if I should go after Theo and tell her that it wasn't working. At that point, I'd probably grovel on my hands and knees, and beg her to return and help me.

I was halfway out the door when I thought I heard a scratchy voice over the radio.

"*I...iden...you....or...*"

My heart flew into my throat and I rushed back over to the microphone.

"Hello? Can you hear me?"

I heard more static, and then the word *Herin*. I was almost dizzy with relief. Herin was a neutral country, friendly to both Kylae and Rave and—

My mouth moved before I could stop it, "I'm here with another Raven soldier. We...we're both Raven. We crashed here on this island..."

I blinked, realizing I knew nothing of where we were on a map. If only Theo were there. She'd know what to do.

I listened for the Herin response, and realized other than the first few scraps, there was nothing.

"Hello?" I called into the microphone. "*Hello?*"

I ducked under the console. Maybe I could rewire the cords and make the signal stronger? I unconnected the wires, then twisted them with other ones Theo had left dangling. I tried several combinations, pulling down other wires and connecting those. None of them worked —and I'd lost track of which ones connected the radio in the first place.

"*Fuck!*"

I pulled myself out and raced around the command room. Completely out of my element, I banged on every button and typed on every keyboard, knowing that it wasn't going to do much good, but hoping that I could figure something out.

I leaned against the console and sighed loudly out of frustration when my gaze landed on a small metal door on the wall. Crossing the room quickly, I opened it to reveal another circuit board with switches and my eyes lit up. To my untrained, hopeful eyes, it was just what I was looking for. I pushed all the switches to the right at the same time. The room was bathed in black for a moment, then red, then back to light. A siren wailed somewhere in the building, before it was joined by the one in the center command. I covered my ears to the loud noise.

"Self-destruct mode engaged."

"Shit."

THEO

My weeks-old leg injuries still handicapped me as I walked, but I was moving on pure fury alone. I hoped I was headed in the right direction that would lead me to camp. The place I would now call home. It was nothing but a clearing, the wreckage of my plane a reminder of how I'd arrived on the island. But I ached for it now. I wanted to be as far away from the graves of my people as possible.

Had they even buried them? Or just burned their bodies like garbage?

I fell to my knees, disgusted and needing to empty my stomach. But I swallowed the sickness. Wasting nutrients was idiotic.

Instead, I watched thick droplets—tears—fall to the ground.

Galian's reaction shouldn't have been surprising. It was easy to see him not as the prince of Kylae, but as the *princeling*. His ignorance of basic survival skills, his lame jokes. The way he ministered to me when I was hurt (and even when I was not). But this place was a stark reminder of the vast ocean that lay between us, filled with blood shed on both sides.

Though significantly more Raven blood than Kylaen.

It gave me some solace that Galian would be able to go home. He would return to his life of princeling bliss. Perhaps find a wife who would bring his ego down a few pegs.

And I would be damned to live on this island with the ghosts of my ancestors.

The island was suddenly alive with wind and rustling, and I imagined a wolf appearing at my side again.

No, I reminded myself, not a wolf. A dog brought there to keep the Raven prisoners in line. Perhaps that was why they'd been so drawn to me that day. They were bred to hunger after Raven flesh.

But Galian had come for me then, just as some part of me hoped he'd come for me now.

I rolled onto my back and looked up at the gray sky. Tears continued to leak down my face as I lay there, letting the ache in my leg pulse. I grieved for the hundreds of innocent Ravens who'd died here. I grieved for myself and how I'd never know anything more than a life of survival.

And I grieved for my short and sweet friendship with Galian. Grieving for what could have been between us if we had never found—

Boom.

The sound reverberated through my entire body. It sounded like an air attack, the thick bombs that I'd hear in my plane. I sat up and looked back at the source of the sound. Fear raced through my veins as a black column of smoke billowed to the sky.

"Galian..."

I hurried back the way I'd come, ignoring the sharp pain in my leg as I used it more than I should have. I'd gone farther than I'd

135 | S. USHER EVANS

thought, or the trek back took longer because I was afraid of what I'd find.

The thick, acrid smoke hit me as I approached the burning former radar station. The walls, the ceiling, even some of the surrounding vines—all of it was dancing in orange flame. Pieces of the building lay scattered around me as well, twisted metal and burning wood.

"G-Galian!" I choked into the smoke. Could I make it through the flames? Was he hurt, trapped under a fallen beam?

Was he already dead?

"Galian!" I cried, inching closer. "Galian, are—"

"Theo?"

I spun around, half-wondering if I had hallucinated. But there he was, his face and hair covered in black ash. In his arms, he carried a singed box.

"Wh-what's that?" I asked, for lack of any other question.

"I set off the alarm," he said, squinting at the fire behind me. "And I wanted to get the important stuff out before it all went up in smoke."

"What important stuff?" I asked.

He opened the box and showed me—blankets, gauze, alcohol. Again, his first thought had been my health. My heart swelled with emotion as I looked at him. In the ten minutes I'd thought I would never see him again, I'd crossed an ocean of grief. Looking at him yanked me across it faster than light and left me breathless.

"I don't know what else we'll be able to get out of there," he said, coming to stand beside me. "Maybe I can go back in—"

I flew into his arms, not even caring that I knocked the box out of his hands, or him back a step. His face went slack with shock, but slowly, his arms wrapped around me, his hand resting at the small of my back.

"I'm okay," he whispered into my hair.

I nodded, knowing he was holding me in a very intimate embrace, and not caring if he wanted to or not. I was crying again, and he slid his hand up and down my back to comfort me.

"I'm sorry," he whispered.

"For what?"

"For...?" He blinked, glancing to the burning wreckage. "For that. All of it. The experiments and the lies and...well, I know you probably never wanted to sleep there again, but it could have been a shelter and—"

"Yeah, how did you manage to blow up the lab?" I asked with a small, incredulous laugh.

"I was trying to..." He sighed deeply, and I felt the sigh reverberate in his chest. He was still holding me as if I were his lover. And then he looked at me as if I were. "I found a Herin channel. I told them we were both Raven."

My breath hitched in my chest. "You...?"

"But then I lost it and I set off the self-destruct mode," he said, releasing me from his embrace. I missed it immediately. "And—"

"Galian." I stepped forward. "Let's go home."

"But—"

"If they are looking for us," I said, tilting my head up to the column of black smoke billowing to the sky. "They can't miss that."

ELEVEN

GALIAN

The radar station burned for two full days. The thick column of black smoke spewing toward the sky was visible from our camp on the other side of the island. But no one came, and this time, I didn't expect them to.

I'd managed to grab three blankets from the lab before everything went up in smoke—which turned out to be a blessing, because when I returned to salvage what I could find, most everything was burnt to a crisp. Though I found the showers blown to smithereens, I did find one working tap, which meant our days of boiling seawater were at an end. Two more trips resulted in nothing but to dirty up my old Kylaen uniform which the both of us still wore.

I didn't ask Theo to come back to the laboratory with me, and she didn't offer. I still had questions about it, more specifically—what the actual fuck was my great-grandfather thinking? Theo, however, always had dinner caught and cooked by the time I returned from scavenging trips. Like so many other things, the atrocities at the lab went undiscussed.

After a few trips to the lab, I uncovered a half-charred mattress, which I decided I would drag back to camp. Unfortunately, the sun had long set by the time I showed up, and I got an earful from Theo about the dangers of being alone at night and how stupid it was to drag something so unnecessary back.

"Yeah, but...eh?" I tossed one of our three blankets on top of it and gestured to her. "Practically the hotel at the Opiela!"

"What's that?"

"The fanciest hotel in Norose," I said, adjusting the blanket on top of the mattress to cover the burned spots. "I mean, compared to sleeping on the ground."

"Galian, I didn't catch anything today!" she said suddenly.

My stomach dropped. I'd become accustomed to eating little, but I didn't like the prospect of not having *anything*.

She wrung her hands nervously. "It's been bad since the explosion. I don't know if we've scared them off or eaten them all or what," she said, plopping down on the mattress. "I need you to stay here and help me."

"Okay," I said, sitting next to her. "We'll figure something out. Don't worry."

There was a new light in her eyes when she looked up at me. A little relief, and a little comfort. It had been a week since the explosion; had she really been worried about that the whole time?

"You know, you don't have to keep that kind of stuff from me," I said with a small shrug. "If you want my help, ask for it."

She didn't respond, but a ghost of a smile turned the corners of her mouth.

"Seriously, Theo." I nudged her gently. "Don't think you've got to handle all of this on your own. I know what I'm doing now. I can handle it."

"Skin a rabbit, and I'll believe that."

"No rabbits here to skin, *Captain*."

That was the wrong thing to say, as the levity on her face melted away. "I'm sorry," she whispered.

"Don't be," I said with a yawn as I lay back on the mattress. It already felt like heaven. "But you get to take the first shift."

All joking aside, the next morning, I was ravenous when I woke and I wished I had spent a little less time dragging the mattress back and more time keeping an eye out for food. And from Theo's snapping, I guessed she was thinking the same.

We traveled due north from camp, walking for an hour before deciding on a spot. I dug holes while Theo set up her rudimentary traps. Once that was complete, we sat side by side, hidden by a low tree, watching our respective traps and itching for the moment to spring.

My stomach moaned loudly, and she shifted beside me. I wasn't sure if it was a sign of annoyance or if she were simply adjusting herself. But my stomach continued to make noises. If we didn't catch something soon, I was going to crack open one of those sixty year old cans of vegetables half-melted up at the station.

I saw movement out of the corner of my eye and spotted a bird flying around. It was small, and would probably give us an ounce of meat each, but it was food.

Then the little asshole landed gently on the trap, picked up the morsel of food, and flew away.

I opened my mouth to curse, but Theo let loose a long string of words I didn't understand.

"What did you say?" I asked.

"Just pissed off," she replied, sitting back and rubbing her stomach. "And hungry."

"Me too, but what did you say? I've never heard those words before."

She half-smiled. "I wouldn't expect you had, princeling. It's the old Raven tongue."

"They still use that over there?"

"There are some words the common language doesn't work for," she replied, pulling herself up and limping over to the trap to reset it. "Like to describe how hungry I am right now."

"But what does it mean?"

She hedged, and I could almost read her mind, wondering if she should share it with me.

"I mean, if it's a state secret..."

"No," she said quicker than I'd expected her to. "No, I'm actually trying to figure out how it's translated."

"It's not a one-to-one?"

"Not really." She shook her head. "I mean, I can literally translate it, but it wouldn't make any sense."

"What is it literally translated?"

She blushed again, and I had no idea what to expect. "I shit in the milk of your whorish mother."

My eyes nearly flew out of my head. "*What?*"

She grinned at my shock. "It's not meant to be taken literally. It's something we say when we're really, *really* pissed off at something."

"I shit in the..." The mental image made me cringe.

"Really, Galian, don't take it literally. Raven words aren't supposed to mean what they literally mean."

I blinked at her in confusion.

"It's hard to explain." She furrowed her brow. "For example, you would call your mother *okaachai*, but it doesn't mean mother." She paused, considering her own words. "I mean, it does, but it means more than just someone who gave birth to you. It means an older female person that cares for you, that you just have this...I don't know." She huffed, obviously annoyed that she couldn't find the right words.

I smiled at her frustration. "Are there any other words?"

"*Osaichai* is father, same thing," she said. "The only person I'd consider an *osaichai* is Lanis. Older guy who looks after you like a father. But I never called him that."

"Why not?"

"Raven words are only used when you feel it in your soul," she said. "You can't just *say* them. You have to *feel* them."

"Well, why don't you *feel* them at me?" I joked.

She glared at me, but there wasn't any heat behind it. "There is another one that's used more commonly, but..." Her face reddened again.

"What is it?"

"*Amichai*," she said, with a pained look on her face. "It means...lover."

I snorted at the way she'd said the word and wondered if she'd ever been in love in her life. "Lover, huh? So like boyfriend or—"

"No, for someone to be your *amichai*, you have to feel it. I've heard that the word just comes out when..." She trailed off, growing more flustered as she tried to think about it.

"When what?" I pressed, enjoying this rare moment of unguardedness. The idea of Theo in love made me smile.

"When you are truly, madly, and unbelievably in love with someone," she said, looking away.

"And who is your ay-mi-k-ai?" I attempted the word, but it

came out clumsily and with a Kylaen accent.

She bristled, but it had nothing to do with the butchering of her word. "I...I've never been in love. Never had time to be."

"Not to break our rule," I said cautiously. "But...does anyone in Rave have the time to be in love?"

"Love? No." Theo shook her head. "But they do put a high priority on having babies. Most girls try to get pregnant so they'll get pulled from the force for a few months."

"Why didn't you...do that?" I asked, hoping I hadn't crossed the line.

"It didn't appeal to me. It seemed like trading one conscription in for another." She smiled brightly. "And to be honest, *nothing* compares to flying."

"Oh, I can think of some things that do." I let a lascivious look cross my face and she growled at me, turning purple in ferocious blush. I suddenly wondered if Theo had ever been with a man before.

"Have *you* ever been in love?" she asked. "And sleeping with Kylaen debutants doesn't count."

I considered the question, not one I'd ever been asked before. "Actually, not really, not like that anyway. I've dated girls but I didn't really...*love* any of them."

"Why not?"

"I don't know," I said with a half-shrug. "I guess I always kind of figured they were only with me because I was 'Prince Galian' or something. They wanted the attention, the cameras, and the fame. They wanted to tell their friends they were dating me."

I waited for her eye roll or smart remark, but there was none. "That sounds lonely."

"You have to understand, my life back in Kylae

is...was...nothing more than a constant barrage of photographers and duties and pressure. If I found someone I liked, they usually hated having their face all over the front page of the Kylaen tabloids, with stories wondering when I was going to marry them or who I was cheating on them with."

That elicited an eyebrow raise. "Did you ever?"

I shook my head violently. "Never. Was never in a relationship long enough. The ones I liked usually left after the first date, and the ones who stuck around tended to be more interested in the attention, and so I ended things pretty quickly."

THEO

He trailed off, staring at our empty trap deep in thought. I'd never considered what it was like to live in that fishbowl. The more I got to know him, the more I became aware of his gentle acceptance. He really didn't let any of the pressures of being a prince affect him, never flaunted his money or his power. Not that he had any of it on the island.

"What?" He'd noticed me watching him and I looked away.

"Nothing," I murmured.

"So, I'm really thinking I want to open one of those cans of expired beans back at the station," he said, and I could practically hear his stomach growling. He had been so good up until now, I was willing to allow him a bit of grumbling. Or perhaps I was still grateful to have him in my life again.

We hadn't spoken about the laboratory or the experiments that Galian had found. I was actively avoiding thinking about it, because it reminded me of that bloody sea between his country and mine. I didn't think there was space in my heart to forgive Kylae for the atrocities and still have room for Galian, so I chose to keep the one I wanted more.

"I think I understand what you mean about those Raven words," he said after a long moment. "I don't consider His Highness to be in the same...league as my mother. He's just...well, he's just the sperm donor, I guess." He flushed a little. "But I've never considered him a father like I consider my mother to be...well, my *mother*."

Something changed in his face when he spoke of the queen—no, his mother. I knew Korina from news reports and interviews about her charities. But to Galian, she was his '*kaachai*.

"What's she like?"

"Who? My mom?"

I nodded, turning to look back out into the forest.

"She's...man, she's something else," Galian said, sounding wistful and it warmed me to hear him so affectionate. "Elegant and kind. Educated. Graceful and patient. Passionate about making Kylae a better place. And yet, she always had time for us. No matter how busy she was. Unlike my father, who was more concerned about..."

I turned to look at him, about to mention that he was close to breaking our "no-war-talk" rule. However, he appeared to need a release. And I supposed that even Prince Galian couldn't speak freely in his own kingdom, so on our island, I would let him talk. Besides, I was a little curious how someone as gentle as Galian could come from someone so heinous. "What's that like? Being the son of Grieg?"

"It's weird. To everyone else, he's His Majesty, but to me, he's just my overbearing and overly critical asshole of a father. He's never let me breathe, you know? I've always been one giant disappointment to him. So, you know, for a while, I thought—hey, why not just give him what he wants."

"The partying?" I offered.

"It wasn't as bad as they made it out to be, but it still felt like I had some sort of control over my own life," he said with a conviction that was unlike him. "But I stopped when I saw what it was doing to my mom, and...well, when she took me to Mael."

I swiveled my head around to stare at him. He spoke so casually, so easily about such a horrible place. "You've *been* there?"

His face was ashen, and it had nothing to do with our hunger. "Yes. My mother wanted to show me what my father was doing, and also, since the photographers were hounding me," he smiled a bit evilly, "I figured it served them right to be forced to go there anyway."

"The place where your father..." I trailed off. I was trying very hard not to pick a fight, so I chose my words carefully. "I don't think anyone *deserves* to go there. Especially the ones imprisoned there."

"I know," he said quietly, and silence descended between us for a moment.

I snuck a glance over at him and saw the anguish on his face. I had known Galian long enough to learn that his eagerness to land a joke sometimes outpaced his empathy.

"Is it as bad as I've heard?" An olive branch, I hoped, to let him know I wasn't cross with him.

"Worse," he whispered. I saw the horror reflected in his eyes. No wonder he took so long to tell me. "The moment I returned to university, I switched my major to pre-med. I had to do something to help someone. And I was pretty good at it until...well...His Royal Dickheaded-ness decided that losing one son wasn't enough."

I stifled a laugh at the name, but Galian was still somber.

"Mom was livid when she found out that I was volun-told to join the military. I'm the youngest, so she's always had a bit of a soft spot for me. Rhys was always with my father, learning how to be a king and all that. And Dig was always a brute, even as a little kid. So she and I, we just...got close."

"Your brothers?" I asked, glancing out at the still-empty traps. "What are they like?"

"Rhys is...all right, I guess," he said. "I wish he'd stand up to my father though. I don't think he realizes that soon *he's* going to be the one making all the decisions. Might be useful to make some now."

I mused silently that Galian chose not to stand up to his father in much the same way. "And your...other brother?"

"Asshole," he said darkly.

"But he's dead," I said, trying to not sound too harsh. "Don't you mourn him? Even a little?"

"It's complicated, Theo." At my quizzical expression, he said, "Look, I loved my brother, just like I love my father. But...you can love someone and not like them very much."

"Why is your father...why is he so intent on reclaiming Rave?" I asked. "Why after all these years?"

"When the war started, it was about resources," he said quietly. "But now...now if the war were to end, half Kylae's economy would be gone. Thousands of our citizens are employed by the armed forces or support staff to the war machine. It's...it's big business. As easy as it would be to stop sending planes over there, it might completely upend the Kylaen economy."

I continued to stare at him, unsure of how I felt about what he'd said. I decided to change the subject. "Tell me more about your brothers."

He nodded with a cautious glance at me. "Dig used to beat the ever-loving shit out of me, and sometimes Rhys would help. I think he always thought I was softer because I spent so much time with Mom. She..." He bristled and a blush crept up his neck. "She had a name for me they always used, too. Mocking me."

The image of Galian as a young child at the mercy of two older brothers was too much, and I couldn't stop the giggle and then the full-blown laughter that bubbled forth.

Galian stared at me like I had two heads. "Was that a *giggle*?"

I covered my mouth to hide the smile on my face. "Nope."

"Theophilia Kallistrate, did you just *giggle* at me?"

"Hey, what did I say about calling me by my full name?" I barked.

"That I can do it all I want if you're laughing at my childhood misery," he retorted.

I wanted to correct him, tell him he didn't know the meaning of childhood misery, but somehow I couldn't. Galian's privileged life was enchanting, and for a brief moment, I allowed myself to forget my own terrible one.

"I'm sorry," I said with as much meaning as I could.

Galian's face shifted again, and I knew he was thinking about things heavier than his brothers. "I just wish there was something I could do, you know?" He sighed. "About Mael. About the war. About everything my father does. I wish I could say it's because it's too hard, too political, too...whatever," he whispered. "But the reason is that I'm too cowardly to stand up to my father. I am afraid of what he would do to me."

GALIAN

I waited for her response, for her angry affirmation that I was every bit the weakling she'd expected me to be. When she didn't voice an opinion, I snuck a look at her. She seemed to be appraising me with that quiet, strategic observation I had come to expect from her. I was still smarting that she had laughed at my misery, and I hoped she didn't find me as weak and insignificant as my brothers did.

"I don't think you're cowardly at all," she said after an excruciating few moments. "I think you just don't realize you have a choice."

I cocked my head at her. "What do you mean, I have a choice?"

"Since I was a kid, I've had a gun to my head telling me what to do," she said.

"Right." I winced at my own complaining. Theo truly had a rough life; my bullying brothers were laughable in comparison. I felt like a fool talking about big brothers and bullies when she'd endured so much more.

"It's okay, Galian," she said, knowing exactly why I was grimacing. It was funny how well she knew me. "My point is that nobody ever gave me a choice about what my life was going to be. And if I ever strayed out of line, I was expendable." She sighed heavily. "But you're a prince. And the only thing you're risking is your father's disapproval."

"You never know what he would do," I said darkly. "He did leave me here to die on the island."

Her mouth fell open and her eyes narrowed, then she looked forward. "You think he knows where you are."

I nodded. "It shouldn't have taken them this long to find me, if they were even looking."

"And you don't think that they'd spare no expense to find the prince of Kylae? Your father wouldn't put all available resources toward finding you?"

"I think he probably told everyone he did, but I doubt he actually tried," I said. "I think he could use my death to reinvigorate the country the same way he did after Dig died. And I think...I think I'm only good to my father dead."

"And what about to yourself? Your country? What good are you to them?"

The question caught me off guard, and at the same time was a predictable one from Theo. She was too busy worrying about the fate of her countrymen to be selfish. And yet again, she'd demonstrated more maturity and selflessness in one sentence than I had in my entire twenty-five years.

"You have an opportunity afforded to very few people," she continued. "The ability to make real, lasting change in this world, stem the tide of war. Save millions of lives. All you have to do is believe you can."

Her faith in me was embarrassing, especially in light of the complete waste of a human being I'd been up until that point. Sure, I had gone to medical school, but looking back on it, that was the easy way out. Twelve hour shifts were nothing in the face of standing up to my father and demanding change. I could have camped out at Mael, I could have campaigned and used my position to force people to pay attention.

The idea was frightening, even from the safety of the island. But it was also a little exciting.

"Do you really believe I can make a difference?" I whispered.

"You saved my life," she said with a look in her eye that captured me for a moment. "You convinced me, a Raven soldier, to not only trust you, but call you a friend."

"Friend?" I said, slightly disappointed.

She caught my tone, but a white fluffy tail redirected her attention. She grabbed my arm to quiet me, and we waited with bated breath as the creature moved closer...and closer...and then...

"*Get it*!"

Twelve

Theo

That night we ate like kings, both of us falling into a drowsed stupor that made staying awake to keep watch a struggle. When I awoke the next morning, I was surprised when Galian asked me to show him how to kill and prepare a rabbit. I'd thought it was an empty gesture, but he was an apt, if not overly-eager student.

His first attempt was atrocious. I would've thought after several weeks of watching me slice and dice animals, his stomach would be stronger. But there was a permanent look of disgust on his face as I showed him how to cut, and each slice seemed to pain him. I assumed, when I fell asleep, that I would continue to be responsible for our meals.

Imagine my surprise the following morning when I woke to the smell of cooking meat. Galian had not only captured two rabbits, but had prepared them as well.

"Breakfast is ready!" He beamed like he was serving eggs and bacon.

I grimaced as I tasted the memory of salty pork on my tongue.

Would I ever see it again?

"Hey, what was that for?" Galian stalked over and folded his arms over his chest. "I swear I cooked it long enough—"

"No, it's fine," I said, looking up at him from the mattress. For as much as I had yelled at him for going so far out of his way to find it, and as much as I hated the people who'd brought it here, I was glad for it. "I was just remembering eggs and bacon."

He was practically drooling as he looked at the sky, ominously overcast. "You know, every morning I would have two eggs, over easy, three strips of bacon, toast, and a carafe of coffee delivered to my room." He looked down at me. "And it's been weeks since I'd remembered that. Thanks, Theo."

"Sorry," I said, stretching and wincing as my leg twinged. I narrowed my eyes at the sky; it definitely looked like rain. "Galian? Do you—" I blinked when a raindrop landed square on my nose.

"Uh-oh."

I heard nothing else, for the deluge began almost immediately. I yelped from the cold of it, realizing exactly how blessed we'd been to have gone this long without having to deal with the weather. Without another thought, I yanked the wool blanket over me. It did a little to keep the cold off, as soon it, too, was soaked.

Galian was a bit more awake than I, and quickly stuffed our other two blankets under the mattress to keep them dry then crawled under the soggy blanket with me.

"Shit," he said, wiping the rain off his face as his wet arm pressed against me. "We should have found a cave or something. Are you okay?"

"It's just rain," I said with a grin. "I won't melt."

"But we may freeze," Galian said. He wrapped his arm around

me and pulled me closer. "You're warm."

I was shocked at his brashness, but couldn't argue with him. It *was* warmer than if we sat apart. With the exception of the times he carried me across the island, we hadn't spent much time in close proximity. At least, we'd never sat like this before, shivering and holding each other trying to keep warm.

He adjusted the wet blanket over us and I settled deeper into the crook of his arm, leaning my head on his shoulder. I could hear his heartbeat, a quick *thump-thump-thump*. His breath was shorter as well, and his eyes were fixed on anywhere but me.

Was I actually making him nervous?

"And I was so excited to have made you breakfast," he said, looking longingly at the fire which the rain had nearly put out. The two half-cooked rabbits were doused and steaming.

"I'm very proud of you," I said, and I meant it. "We'll cook the meat once the rain stops."

He flashed me a grin that made my whole body warm. A small voice in the back of my mind reminded me that we were still there together, and there was still a chance for an us. But whether or not I was brave enough to broach the subject was another story.

The rain was cold, I was now completely wet, but I couldn't find much to complain about. I let myself drift back to sleep, smiling a little more when he rested his cheek on my forehead.

GALIAN

It rained for most of the day, but I didn't really mind. After my body got used to the cold and the wet, I could only think about how she felt under my arm, leaning against me. When she woke, she stayed there while we waited out the rain.

We had another easy conversation. She told me about the time she'd adopted a cat in the orphanage and spent all night in the rain looking for it. I told her a story about my favorite teddy bear as a child, and how my asshole older brother threw it into the ocean. We talked more about my mom, and summers at her familial estate in the south of Kylae, and she told me she'd never learned how to swim.

"I'll teach you, if you want," I said. "We have plenty of ocean."

She shivered. "Do you think that would be a good idea? I'm cold enough as it is."

"Okay, next heatwave, you're learning how to swim," I said with a grin.

"Do you think...we'll be here forever?" Her voice was quiet and reflective. I didn't detect any note of fear in it. In fact, she sounded...happy about the idea.

"I hope not."

She had the look I'd grown so accustomed to, the one that told me she was carefully weighing her words. "This is the freest I've ever been in my entire life." She said it breathlessly, like it was some secret she'd been holding onto.

"How so?"

"I've always had to do what other people asked of me. And being here...all I do is for my own survival, and it's...it's the best feeling in the world." She sighed happily. "And I just...I never want it to end, you know?"

I sat back and considered her words. I missed my bed and my morning breakfast and the thought of coffee was enough to give me a small erection. Or perhaps being so close to her was doing it. I quickly directed my thoughts to something else.

"There's nothing about the island that you like?" she asked.

"Well, there aren't tabloid photographers chasing me all over the place," I admitted with a grimace. That was nice, although I wondered what kind of stories they were running about me now. Probably still mourning my supposed death. "You don't miss anything about Rave? What about your family? Friends?"

She shrugged. "I don't have any. Not really. After I was conscripted, I made some friends at flight school, but we were all assigned to different squadrons and bases. And I tried..." She took a long breath. "I tried to not get too attached to anyone in my squadron."

I held her a little tighter to comfort her, unsure of what I should say. I don't think there was a good response to that.

When the rain lessened to a hazy mist, I got up to rebuild our fire to keep cooking our food. The second we disconnected, I felt like I'd jumped into an ice bath. I hurried as I gathered kindling and tried to start it.

"W-we n-need to f-f-find a better sh-shelter," Theo said through chattering teeth.

I nodded in agreement, striking the rocks together faster. I realized that the wet twigs wouldn't catch fire, but perhaps the dry wool blankets would. I hurried back to the mattress and lifted it.

"W-w-what are you looking for?" Theo asked.

"Dry kindling," I said. "I might have to sacrifice one of our blankets."

"W-w-w-why n-n-not use the t-twigs?" she said, pointing a shaking finger to the bone dry sticks and leaves under the mattress.

"Because you're smarter than I am," I said, grabbing them and putting them back on the fire pit. In short order, I had a small fire growing, and Theo joined me to warm her blue hands.

"You okay?" I asked.

"Yes," she whispered. "I-I don't know if I-I'll ever be w-warm again."

I slid around to the other side of the fire and wrapped my arms around her wet frame. Quickly, I ran my hands up and down her back to create warmth, but she continued to shiver.

"It might be better if you get out of your wet clothes," I said, standing and pulling out one of the dry blankets. She nodded and unzipped the soaking uniform, letting it fall to the ground. I tried not to stare at the now-translucent white bra and underwear that stuck to her body as I wrapped the dry blanket around her. She continued to shiver, so I tried to pull her into my arms.

"Y-you're wet too," she said.

I hadn't even noticed anymore, my concern over her outweighing my own misery. But when she mentioned it, cold seeped in through every inch of my skin.

"C'mon," she whispered, opening the blanket a little in invitation. I was so cold that I immediately unzipped my soaking wet jumpsuit and let it fall off.

"Um." Theo's face grew red as she stared at me, and for a moment, I was stunned by her sudden modesty. Until a cold breeze fluttered past my naked ass.

When we'd arrived at the lab, I'd exchanged my disgusting clothes for a fresh set of Kylaen uniforms. But the explosion happened before I'd had a chance to wash my filthy boxers, so I'd been making do without any underwear.

Something I'd forgotten when unceremoniously disrobing in front of Theo.

Her gaze danced around at everything but me. I wanted to make fun of her but she was so flustered and cold that I didn't have the heart. Instead, I plucked our clothes off the ground and hung them over a tree then grabbed the other dry blanket and wrapped it around myself.

Theo was still staring at the ground as if she'd seen something truly shocking.

"I hope I'm not offending your delicate Raven sensibilities," I teased.

She scowled and sat down on the mattress, wrapping her blanket tighter around herself. "I just wasn't expecting to see a dick, that's all," she replied and it excited me a little that she'd focused on that part of my anatomy. "Could've warned me."

I laughed and joined her on the mattress, cozying up next to her. I was a little bit hurt when she inched away.

"I'm sorry. I actually forgot I wasn't wearing anything," I said, hoping I hadn't truly offended her. "It was cold, and..."

She smirked. "*Little* cold, huh?"

"Fuck off."

THEO

It wasn't that I had never seen a man's genitals before. It wasn't that I was uncomfortable with nudity. It wasn't even that he'd surprised me.

It was that I had been thinking about him nonstop for the past few nights, and seeing him naked was so damned tempting that I had to employ every single piece of restraint to keep my hands to myself. Especially after falling asleep in his arms, I was so aroused that seeing all of him was almost painful. And although I'd quipped about it being cold, there was nothing small about him.

We sat wrapped in our respective blankets and waited for our clothes to dry. Galian stared ahead, lost in thought as he so often was. I took in the sight of him, and how much he'd changed since we'd been on the island. His beard, once adorably sparse, and now fully grown in, aged him somewhat, erasing the baby face that had so often graced the cover of gossip magazines. In my opinion, he was more attractive now than dressed in his finest tuxedo.

And there I was, sitting next to this handsome man, wrapped in nothing but a blanket, and frozen in indecision about whether or not I should make the first move. Then again, I'd never "made a move" in my life. I could command a squadron and make strategic decisions with the lives of others. I could trap and kill a rabbit.

But romance? Sex? I was as green as Galian had been when we first landed on the island. I hadn't had time for flirting and boys, so I didn't consider myself very good at it.

Yet, I was already flirting with him, I supposed. I'd made him laugh; he'd made me laugh. We'd talked about topics ranging from his family to my childhood to how well our traps were performing. Was that flirting? Was that enough to entice him into bed with me?

And did I just want him in bed, or did I want something more?

When we decided that the gray clouds were too ominous to ignore, we slid on the sticky damp clothing, ate the two rabbits Galian had cooked, and set off to find a more permanent shelter.

We chose an eastern path, pausing to check under every shaded tree and bush for suitable shelter. Twice, we saw what I thought was another feral dog, but it disappeared before I could get a good look at it. Besides, Galian had his flare gun stuffed into the waist of his pants with our last flare, should we encounter anything that wanted to eat us.

I began to fall behind, and Galian asked several times if I wanted him to carry me. I told him I didn't need his help to walk, but the truth was that I needed some space between us. He trudged on ahead, and I watched the wet uniform stick to his muscles. He was thinner than when we'd landed on the island, but still beautiful. I was enjoying my view, until he complained about me walking too slowly and decided, unilaterally, that he was going to carry me on his back.

Now, of course, the problem was that I had my hands around his shoulders, I could feel the muscles move under my breasts. And with my legs splayed across his back, my ability to focus on finding shelter was decidedly hampered. Every time he adjusted me, a jolt of pleasure ran up my spine. More than once, I stared at his neck, his lips, mine only inches away, wondering what he tasted like.

Galian stumbled over a root, bringing me back to our search for shelter. It had sprinkled a little while ago, and we'd be in for another rough night if we didn't find something soon.

I thought, a bit hopefully, that we may have to use each other for warmth again.

Somewhere in the more intelligent side of my brain, I knew I shouldn't be indulging in this silliness. Finding better shelter was crucial to our survival. The rain was coming again, and we needed to be warm.

But my brain refused to cooperate. Nineteen years of being the responsible, strong one, and I was finally done with it. I wanted to be a silly girl with a crush on a boy.

I turned to look at my carrier again. Galian was uncharacteristically focused, his brow furrowed and his face stony. I wondered what he was thinking about.

GALIAN

I thought I was going to die with Theo on my back. It was a good thing she couldn't see down the front of me, because I had an erection so big that it made it hard to walk. The feel of her breasts against my back, the way her thighs tightened around my waist, her breath on my neck. I kept envisioning pulling her off, tossing her on the ground, and doing things to her that made my erection even worse.

I adjusted her again on my back, more so I could discreetly arrange the bulge in my pants. She squeaked a little, and it sent more blood to my crotch. God, but I wanted to hear her make that noise for me.

"Think it'll rain?" I asked, hoping conversation would help me refocus.

"Mm."

I sighed; of all the times for Theo to get quiet.

"The war sucks, doesn't it?" I tried, desperate for release. Maybe we could get into an argument, maybe she'd get furious at me and I'd stop thinking about burying my head in her breasts.

"Absolutely."

I wish I could get into your pants. "I miss having a shower."

"Me too."

Damn, now I was thinking about her in the shower before the laboratory exploded. Bad conversation topic.

"So what else is new?"

"What in God's name are you doing?" she asked.

"I'm making conversation," I said. *And trying to get rid of this need to be inside you.*

"Why?"

"Because it's too quiet."

"Perhaps, then, you should focus on finding a place for us to stay, or we should go back to camp." She sounded angry with me. I didn't care. She'd be a lot angrier at me if she found out what I was thinking about her.

"And sit in the rain again?" I asked with a snort. I'd sit in the rain for years if it meant I could be naked with her. "Weren't you the one who suggested we find shelter?"

"Why are you snapping at me?" she asked.

"Why are you snapping at *me*?"

She didn't have an answer, and I chalked it up to hunger and being cold and wet. For me, I was tired, cold, wet, and sexually frustrated.

THEO

I was tired, cold, wet, and sexually frustrated. It didn't help that Galian kept adjusting me on his back, and there was now a painful throbbing in that sensitive part of my body. And it definitely didn't help that I was completely transfixed on him, instead of on the topic at hand. I was effectively useless, a besotted idiot.

And as my stomach rumbled, I remembered that we'd eaten our breakfast this morning and, because I was with Galian instead of hunting for more, we would go hungry tonight.

"Put me down," I insisted, pushing off him. He didn't argue and I stumbled back a little.

"What's wrong?"

"I'm headed back to camp." It wasn't a total lie; we did need to catch dinner before it got too dark. But I also needed to get away from him before I did something stupid. I began to walk when I heard Galian's amused chuckle behind me.

"We didn't come that way," Galian said with a small smile. "Were you not paying attention?"

My face nearly burst into flames. "I was, but..."

"See?" He pointed to the mark on the tree. "I've been marking the trees. They'll lead you back."

"I *knew* that," I said with more than my usual amount of heat. "But I was just—"

The ground crumbled beneath my feet and I slid downward on a bed of pebbles and stones, my scream echoing in the darkness. I came to a stop after just a few short, heart-stopping seconds. I winced as I moved, but I'd been lucky to slide down the whole way on my tailbone. Though my backside didn't agree.

"Theo!" Galian's voice echoed above me. "Theo, are you all right?"

"I'm fine," I coughed in the dusty air.

Light filtered into the cave as Galian moved more brush out of the way. The slope I'd slid down was maybe six feet, and flat enough that Galian could crawl down to join me. The cave was stone and sturdy, no chance of it falling in on us. And was exactly the kind of place we needed.

"Ow," I winced. My tailbone was now added to the list of things that ached.

Galian reached down and helped me stand. "Are you all right?" he asked again. "Seriously?"

"Nothing bruised but my pride," I said, dusting myself off.

In this small space, we had to stand much closer together than usual, our arms brushing. There was hardly enough room to walk, although I was fairly sure we could fit our mattress and maybe a few other things.

"I might be able to dig more of this out," Galian said, running his hands along the slope. "Or maybe add a little ladder or something like that." He looked down at me again with a pleased sort of smile. "So what do you think? Is this a good home for us?"

I blinked at his choice of words. *Home.* A smile crossed my face. "Yeah, I think this'll do nicely."

Thirteen

Galian

The first night we spent in the cave, Theo must've decided that we no longer needed to worry about predators killing us in our sleep. For that night, she joined me on the mattress that I'd dragged to the cave, curled into a ball, and fell asleep before I could question her. The second night was the same, as was the third. By the fourth night, I got a small smile and a "goodnight," which I took to mean she was at least not disgusted by the idea of sharing a bed with me. But I didn't want to push things further. She was sleeping next to me, but sleeping *with* me would be an entirely different question.

Once we'd settled in our new cave, things became a lot more routine. Before then, we'd just been living day-to-day, simply trying to survive. But days were passing in the blink of an eye, routine slowly overcoming the ever-present worry that we would not live to see the next day.

I'd wake first and catch breakfast, waking Theo up with the smell of roasted meat. After breakfast, I'd start working on whatever project that had piqued my interest while Theo found lunch. In the afternoons, it was my turn to find food while Theo tinkered on a new trap. Some days, I wasn't sure that we said two words to each other, but every night, we curled up in our cave next to one another and slept soundly.

One of my more pressing projects was the hunt for something other than Goddamned rabbit. Theo made no mention that she was tired of it, but I could barely stand the taste of it anymore. My options were either the birds we heard chirping high in the trees, or what we could catch in the sea. I had begun to consider options for fishing poles. On a trip back to our original camp, I'd found my old parachute on the beach, which meant I had a fishing line. But a hook was a different story. I considered many different options, from branches to using the metal pieces on my shoes. It wasn't until I ventured back to the laboratory that I found something useful—a box of metal sutures.

"Hey, it's not much, but it's worth a shot!" I said to Theo's dubious face when I told her of my plan. She shrugged and continued sharpening the knife with a nearby rock.

The shore of the Madion Sea was a short walk from our cave, and I carefully carried my makeshift pole and line to the edge of the water. I stood at the shore and flung the end of the suture-line into the water.

"Here," Theo said, appearing by my side. She pulled the line back to her and stuck a small piece of rabbit on the end.

"Thanks," I said, grinning.

"I still don't think this is going to work," she said, glancing out to the water. "You'd have to get farther out. I doubt fish come this close to shore."

"What about that?" I said, pointing behind her to a rocky outcropping. "I could stand up there and toss it in?"

I felt her unsure gaze as I jogged over to the rock and climbed up the rocky cliff face. The task was made more difficult by the fishing pole in my hand, but I made it. I stood and looked out upon the island, including Theo, who stood some thirty feet below me.

"I think I like you better with two feet on the ground," she said. "Please be careful up there."

"Just let me try this for a bit," I said, picking up the pole and reaching back to cast the line out. My foot slipped and I knew I was falling. I saw the rock speeding towards me. The last thing I remembered was Theo screaming my name.

THEO

His body fell in slow motion, and I heard myself scream his name, followed by the sickening crack that echoed somewhere in the bottom of my stomach. I scrambled over to him as quickly as I could, flipping him over in the rocky sand.

"Galian! *Galian*!" I shook him then stopped, unsure if it would harm him or wake him. "*Galian!*"

His eyes remained shut, his body motionless except for the small rise and fall of his chest. I pressed my hands to his ribcage to feel his heartbeat. But that didn't change the fact that he looked dead.

"Okay, if you're playing with me," I said in a shaky voice, "it's not funny anymore. Time to wake up and laugh about it. You got me, princeling."

I waited for his eyes to pop open, for his cheesy, smug grin, but none of it came. He was truly unconscious, and I had absolutely no idea what to do.

"Galian, I need you to wake up and tell me what I have to do," I whispered helplessly. Panic bubbled up, but I calmed myself so I wouldn't lose my head. That, at least I was trained for.

I considered all Galian had done for me in our weeks on this island. When we'd first crashed, he had cleaned my wounds with rubbing alcohol and made sure they were wrapped. But his injuries appeared internal, aside from a small cut on his forehead and what I assumed would be a large bruise.

I glanced down at him again, shaking him gently to see if I could rouse him to consciousness. When he didn't move, panic rose again, and I forced it down.

"What would Galian do," I whispered to myself. Then, in a flash of lightning. "The bag!" Galian's bag, with all his medicine, was back in our original campsite. Maybe I'd find something in it.

But it was all the way on the other side of the island.

I turned behind me to the forest and knew there was no other choice. I needed to get Galian to a safe place first, so I grabbed him under the arms and dragged him. It took me a while, what with my broken leg and his dead weight—a lot heavier than I'd expected—but, grunting, panting, sweating, I finally pulled him down into the cave and onto the mattress.

I collapsed next to him, dripping sweat in exertion and watching his still form. I half-expected him to turn over and settle in, as he did when he was falling asleep at night. When he didn't, I took a few extra moments to make sure he was covered and, I hoped, comfortable.

"Okay, so...stay here."

I waited for him to argue with me. My eyes pricked with tears.

But now was not the time to cry over him. Now I needed to get help.

Before I'd gone five steps, I realized I had no idea where I was on the island. It had been weeks since we'd left our old campsite, and with my leg still healing, Galian had made most of the cross-island treks.

"Think, *kallistrate*." I'd been in worse situations before and managed to keep my head better than this. Then again, my fears up in the sky were about my own survival, whereas now I was concerned for someone else.

My buzzing internal monologue continued until I processed that I wasn't just staring at a tree, but a small mark in the tree. Galian had been marking the trees every few feet! I silently thanked that brilliant princeling as I passed the first mark, running my hand along the grove in the wood.

I walked until I thought I was traveling in circles until I saw it— the wreckage of my plane. I made a beeline for the black bag on the ground. I pulled the bag strap over my shoulder and scavenged our former home for anything else that might help him.

As I fretted around the campsite, I kept wondering why I was making such an irrational fuss over him. Some part of my brain knew he would wake up soon. And if he didn't, that would be the better for me because...

My humanity prevented me from finishing that thought. Galian couldn't die. Galian *wasn't* going to die.

The forest was dark from the thick clouds and impending dusk when I set off back to our cave. I made sure to check every tree for the mark Galian had etched into it. Each one was a reminder of him, warming me. But my leg and my strength wouldn't allow me to go much faster than a slow hobble. Although I could walk short distances on it, traveling back and forth across the island was causing me great pain.

Just as darkness had almost fully descended, I spotted our cave, or rather, I spotted the dwindling fire he'd started hours ago. I rushed to the cave, hoping to see Galian sitting up with a smile on his face.

But he lay in the darkness exactly where I had left him.

Trembling, I knelt down beside him and pressed my hand to his chest, relieved that it rose and fell gently against my skin.

"I'm back," I whispered into his ear. "In case you feel like waking up now."

He didn't move.

"I brought you something," I said, feeling only slightly idiotic for speaking with no one to answer me.

I dumped the bag on the ground and scoured through the tubes and medicines that tumbled out. Our fire had grown dangerously low, and I could barely see the nose in front of my face.

"Stay here," I said to Galian, as I stood to find more kindling.

I barely noticed my leg throbbing from the exertion as I gathered more wood. Soon the light was shining all the way to the back of the cave.

Galian never stirred once. I rested for a moment, hunger and pain and exhaustion gnawing at me. But I couldn't stay still.

I sorted through the medication, reading each one and trying to figure out what they were for. Antiseptic, antacid, antihistamine, anti-itch cream. His cut had scabbed over, and I doubted that he needed a stomach settler or allergy medication.

I looked around the cave at the mess I'd made of his medical supplies and felt even more helpless than before I'd left.

I plopped down on the mattress next to him and ran my hands

through his hair, more to comfort myself than him. His hair was greasy, but then again, so was mine. I didn't care though, I kept running my hands through it. All I wanted in that moment was for him to wake up, to tease me for making such a big deal over nothing. To smile at me with that twinkle in his eye.

I was so overwhelmed, tired, hungry, and worried about him that tears leaked down my cheeks. The release felt good, even though I knew crying would help no one. But there was nothing else I could do but wait. And cry.

As gently as I could, I pulled him into my arms, his head resting in the crook of my neck. His body was warm against mine, further proof that he wasn't dying.

In that moment, holding him in my arms, I realized that I could survive the island without him. I'd walked back and forth to the camp, I'd carried supplies. I was adept at hunting and finding food. I could stomach going to the laboratory every few days to gather water. I could live for months or even years alone.

But as I held Galian close to me, praying he would wake up with every breath I took, I realized I didn't want to be there without him.

Because I loved him.

The realization poured through me like a river, awe-inspiring and terrifying at once. I had never felt so deeply about someone as I felt about the man in my arms. I'd thought I knew love—I had thought I'd loved my plane, maybe even Lanis. But this new feeling was overwhelming and beautiful and like nothing I'd ever felt before.

I tentatively pressed my lips to his, tasting my own tears, and wishing that his lips would respond in kind. It was not how I wanted our first kiss to go, but it was a start. I told myself it was practice for when he awoke and kissed me for real.

"I...I love you," I whispered, testing the words. They sounded silly coming out of my mouth and yet full of weight. I said it again, bolder, and then again, with all the emotion I felt towards him.

I glanced down at his sleeping face and scowled. "If you're just pretending to be asleep to listen to me make a fool of myself..."

But there was no smirk, no smile. No sign of my Galian.

I kissed him again, lingering on his lips and wondering how they could be so soft after all of the hardships we'd gone through. Nothing but his soft breathing informed me he was alive. I lifted my lips again, and more tears fell.

"Galian, I'm kissing you. Please wake up," I whispered through my tears. "Please wake up so I can tell you that I love you."

I pressed his forehead into the crook of my neck, wondering if the closeness would wake him. But he lay limp against me, his warm breath sticky on my chest. So I lay back with him and prayed with every inch of me that we hadn't survived this long—I hadn't fallen in love with him despite all my prejudices and hatred of his people—just for him to die in my arms.

GALIAN

I opened my eyes then squeezed them back together, the light splitting my already pounding head in two. I rubbed my forehead gingerly, registering the scab on the upper right temple. Squinting, I glanced around to register a rocky overhang, the softness under my head, the wool blanket covering my body.

My eyes opened again as memory rushed through me. "Well, that explains the headache," I mumbled to myself.

"Y-you're awake!" Theo's voice echoed from somewhere far away. Before I could respond, she was by my side, fussing and fretting over me as if truly concerned about my health. I looked up at her face, which was streaked with tears.

Tears? Had she been crying over me?

"I'm fine," I said, even though I wasn't really. "How long was I out?"

"I was so worried about you," she said, ignoring my question completely. She moved her fingertips across my skin as if they'd had plenty of practice. Even with my headache, my skin tingled at her touch.

"How's your head?" she asked.

"Hurts," I said, sitting up.

"Please, don't," she said, pushing me gently back down. "You need to rest. I'll be right back." She stood and stared at me for a moment, relief evident in her eyes, then disappeared out of the cave.

To my left, I noticed the black bag that Dr. Maitland had sent with me tossed on the ground. She had pulled out anything and everything left in it and scattered it around the cave. I reached over and picked up one of the small medicine packets and grumbled. Antacid wouldn't help me much.

She reappeared by my side with no less than a pound of rabbit meat. I smiled thinly, not the least bit hungry at the moment. She watched me as if she believed I'd pass out the second she looked away.

"Theo, I'll be fine," I assured her, leaning back into the mattress.

She didn't move, so I took the meat she was offering and took the smallest of bites to show her I was eating. The worry on her face eased slightly.

"Did you eat?" I asked.

She shook her head. "You need it more than—"

I cut her off and handed her the stick. "Eat. You look like hell."

She frowned as she gently took the food from me, and I could tell I'd said something wrong. But it was the truth—she was pale, there were dark bags under her eyes, and she looked...

Like she'd spent the past however-long-I-had-been-asleep scared that I was going to die. Theo had been worried about me all this time. Crying over my probably lifeless-looking body. I could just imagine her desperation, her fear at seeing me unconscious.

And I'd just woken up and said she looked ugly. Score one for the princeling.

"I...I'll go see if I can catch something else," she mumbled, standing up to leave me and my big mouth in the cave.

FOURTEEN

THEO

I stood outside the cave and rubbed the tear streaks off my face. I felt like a fool. Somewhere in the back of my mind, I'd expected Galian to wake up and...what? Sweep me into his arms? Tell me he loved me as much as I loved him? The idea was as laughable as my behavior had been over the past few hours.

I'd fallen for him, but what was to say he felt the same about me? Could I say to his face the same things I'd spoken to his sleeping form? What would his reaction be when I told him? Could I even summon the courage to tell him?

Then of course, there was the concern of *what the hell was I thinking, falling in love with the son of my enemy?*

Behind me, he crawled out of the cave, clutching his forehead and groaning. The urge to ask him if he was well enough to stand bubbled up, but I bit my tongue. He, too, looked like he wanted to say something to me, but didn't. The more time passed, the more idiotic I felt. Nothing had changed between us, and yet everything had changed for me.

"I caught enough food for today," I announced louder than I'd meant to.

"That's...good," he said, rubbing his head. "Find any painkillers while you were out there?"

"N-no," I said, glancing away. He'd given all he had to me during our first few days on the island. My embarrassment deepened that I'd considered Galian's attentiveness anything other than his doctorly duty. I suddenly needed to get away from him. "But I think I'll go fetch some water from...that place."

Galian glanced over, curious. I hadn't set foot near the laboratory since it burned to the ground, sending Galian to refill our water every few days.

"Do you want me to go with you?"

"Should you be moving around after taking such a fall, Doctor?" I asked, swallowing the *princeling*. I shouldn't tease him anymore. It was too close to flirting, and that needed to stop.

"There's water here," he said, picking up one of the plastic bottles. "Seems like this'll last a day or so."

I glanced up at the sky, grateful it was still overcast. "Might storm. Better to get it now than wait."

"Then wouldn't it be better for you to stay here?"

I glowered in his direction and he took a step back. I rationalized that if he were angry with me, he might be less friendly, and then I could begin to detangle my attachment to him. That, at least, would be easier than admitting feelings that he might not share.

I trudged toward the forest but, before I'd gone too far, he called my name. I turned only slightly to see what he wanted.

He stared at the ground and rubbed his head, though I wasn't sure if from pain or awkwardness. "Thanks for...well, for...looking after me."

"I was simply returning the favor," I snapped, turning back. "Now you've saved my life twice, and I've saved yours once."

"But you told me your name," he offered with a hint of amusement, and my heart jumped at the memory. "I thought we agreed that counted for something."

I kept walking. "It doesn't."

"Theo, I'm sorry I said you were ugly."

"What?" I finally spun around to look at him.

"I said you were ugly," he said, an adorably earnest look on his face. "When I woke up, I said you looked rough, and that was...uncalled for. You're obviously mad about that and—"

"I'm not mad at you for that," I blurted out and immediately regretted it. Being mad at him for something so petty would've been easier to explain, because I had no idea why I was angry at him at all.

"Then why are you mad?" Galian asked, a hint of a whine in his voice.

"I... Because you..." I stammered like an idiot. Angry at myself, I balled up my fist and exploded at him. "*What the hell were you thinking, climbing up there? We have enough trouble staying alive without you trying to hasten our demise!*"

He stared at me, shell-shocked.

"I'm going to get water," I finished, already regretting my words. "Try not to die before I get back, *princeling*."

GALIAN

Shame and embarrassment flooded my cheeks. Had I really reverted to the idiot princeling I'd been when I first landed on the island? Theo was right; I shouldn't have been so reckless. But I'd wanted to do something special for the both of us.

And now thanks to whatever had pissed her off, she could barely stand to be in the same cave as me.

I leaned against the cave and poked at the fire, rubbing my sore head and trying to block out the pain. I glanced at the pile of medicine on the ground and searched through it again, finding nothing of value. Still, the ache in my head was starting to ease from a pounding hammer to a dull thud, so I counted that as a win.

With my pain subsiding, I was now left with the uncomfortable knowledge of Theo's anger. It bothered me more than I would've thought possible, much like when I'd done something to disappoint my mother. It wasn't simply her dislike—plenty of people disliked me, it went hand-in-hand with being a prince, but Theo was different. I'd finally earned her respect, and with one slip of my feet, I'd tossed it all away.

But, my brain asked, *is her respect all I want?*

I had grown to care for her very much. Our first day on the island, she hadn't believed I was a doctor, and to soothe my ego, I'd wanted to show her all I knew. What had started out as a deep-seated need to salve my wounded pride had turned into a genuine concern for her wellbeing.

She had awoken something in me—a need to be better than I was. It was no longer about being more than the "princeling," she made me want to return to my country to be a better leader, to right my father's wrongs. I had known what my forefathers' actions had done, but Theo had made those consequences real and tangible. The nameless prisoners I'd seen at Mael were human beings, the same way Theo lived and breathed and thought and cried.

I wanted the war to stop, for Rave to become a great country. To stop sending their children to war and start growing and thriving. If only because Rave was synonymous now with Theo, and I wanted all those things for her.

I felt safe with her. I had told her things I'd never told anyone else, not even my mother. Perhaps it was the sanctuary of the island, but she'd stirred some of my deepest secrets and fears, allowing them to come loose. I wanted her to see the whole of the person I was...because I'd fallen in love with the whole of her.

A long breath left my chest and my heart skipped a beat.

That was it then.

I loved her.

I loved Theo Kallistrate.

"Huh."

THEO

I knew that love made a person irrational, but my behavior was astonishing. I was angry for no reason, looking at him had taken me to the verge of tears, and my brain could barely keep two thoughts straight.

I laughed at myself. I must've really had it bad.

I used to scoff at the girls in my unit when they pronounced their love (usually along with their pregnancy). I hadn't been able to imagine a time when I could value something above my own survival and my country, but now...now my focus was on the both of us. I wanted him to survive more than myself.

I glanced back the way I had come, hoping that Galian might have thought to forgive my lunacy and come after me. I knew I would have to face him eventually and apologize for my horrible behavior. Perhaps he'd just forgive me and not ask me to explain. We could go back to simply surviving and not have to worry about things like whether or not I loved him and if I could ever tell him.

In any case, it didn't do either of us any good for me to lose my head. I had learned that lesson the hard way once already, and it...

I looked around for the tree marks and saw none.

"Shit, *kallistrate*," I growled to myself.

I had gotten myself lost, yet again, because I was too worried about things like love and Galian to pay attention to where I was going.

"How I survived nineteen years is a God-damned miracle," I hissed to no one in particular.

I wasn't even sure how long I had been walking at that point. I glanced up at the sky, noting the direction of the sun. That, at least, could get me closer to the shore, eventually either closer to—

I heard movement behind me.

"Galian?"

No answer.

I glanced up at the sun again. If I kept pushing forward towards it—

Another movement caught my attention.

"Galian, if that's you, I'm sorry," I said, hoping that it *was* Galian and not something else entirely. "I overreacted and shouldn't have yelled at you. Let's head back to the cave and—"

The soft growl from the trees sent my hopes nosediving into my stomach. A wolf emerged from the darkness, creeping towards me with a hungry look that said it hadn't had a good meal in a while. I swallowed hard and took a step back, bumping into a tree.

I glanced up and saw a nearby branch close enough for me to grab. With an eye on the approaching beast, I wrapped my hands around the branch.

The dog lunged, and I scrambled just out of its reach.

It snapped and jawed at me, jumping as I climbed to a higher branch. I was now nearly ten feet off the ground, all of my extremities pulled tightly to me, and praying to God that dogs couldn't climb.

The dog put both paws on the branch and snapped its jaws at me, drool dripping from white fangs. But as much as it jumped, it couldn't reach me on the branch.

My only options were praying Galian would show up and do something to scare it away, or hoping the dog would get bored and leave me.

I heard movement in the brush and swallowed. "G-Galian? Is that you?"

Three more dogs emerged.

"Fuck."

GALIAN

I debated going after her all afternoon, but it wasn't the best idea to move too much until my headache had subsided. Instead, I puttered around our camp, putting all my medical supplies back in the bag, arranging our mattress and blankets, tending to the fire. The busywork made me even more restless, especially as the hours ticked on.

By the time the sun was low in the sky, I knew either Theo was really, really pissed at me, or something was wrong. Either way, I was tired of waiting around. I made sure to tuck our knife and flare gun into my pocket, covered the fire, and set off, calling Theo's name.

I plodded along the path of the marked trees, calling every few minutes for Theo. I wondered what I was going to say when I finally found her. Was she really that pissed off at me? And if so, how could I fix it? Probably grovel, if I'd had to guess. I'd never had to beg for forgiveness before, so I wasn't really sure what it entailed. Knowing Theo, she would make me work for it.

I grinned. Challenge accepted.

Above all, I was pretty sure that I was going to tell her that I loved her. After all, we were surviving day to day, and it wasn't smart to keep secrets like that. Not that I'd ever been one for keeping anything to myself anyway.

The problem was that I couldn't find her.

I walked all the way to the laboratory using the marks I'd made on the trees, and there was no sign of her. By the time I walked back to the old campsite, it was dangerously dark.

I cupped my hands around my mouth and called for Theo again, waiting for the echo of my voice to die down and listening for her reply. When there was none, I considered my options. She might be back at the campsite, but that was unlikely. She might be lost, which was more plausible. Or she could be hurt, which meant I needed to find her before something else did.

Going any further without a light was a bad idea. I could just hear Theo's response if she found me traipsing around in the dark.

"*Princeling, you can't see in the dark. What were you thinking? Idiot.*"

Though I could spend the night there at the old campsite, I didn't want to be separated from her for the night. I stumbled around for a moment, and my foot caught on something—the old, gross blanket we'd used before we'd found better ones in the laboratory.

I quickly made a small fire in our old pit and used the light to find a large stick. Gingerly, I wrapped the blanket around the stick and lit it on fire. It burned pretty nicely for me, but I knew I wouldn't have much time before it went out.

Holding the light above my head, I braved the darkening woods, calling Theo's name.

THEO

Three dogs had turned into five, and now what I presumed was the entire pack of Raven-eating beasts sat at the foot of the tree, salivating and waiting for me to come down. To make matters worse, the sun was gone, and night had fallen, leaving my options limited to simply stay in the tree forever or try to figure something else out.

I'd called for Galian until my voice was hoarse, but I must've been on the other side of the island, or, worse, he was still angry with me for yelling at him and had given up. At this point, I was simply hoping he wouldn't come stumbling into this mess.

I pulled off a nearby limb and threw it as hard as I could. Three of the dogs left, but the rest of the pack didn't budge. The dim light reflected off their dripping fangs and I sighed.

"*Theo!*"

"Galian!" I cried, nearly falling off my perch in the tree.

"*Theo! Where are you?*"

"Galian, get out of here!" I screamed as the wolves perked up.

"Theo!" His voice came closer, and I saw an orange glow in the distance. "Theo, where are you? I'm sorry for—"

"Galian!" I screamed as more wolves stood, noses twitching and soft growls rumbling from below. "Galian, you have to listen—go back to the camp and stay there!"

He appeared next to my tree and took a step back, the dwindling light of his torch illuminating his face. "Theo, where are you?"

"Up here," I said dully. "You were supposed to go away."

"And what? Leave you for wolf-food?" He stuck his torch, now just red embers on the stick, into the ground. The fire was enough of a distraction to keep the wolves at bay as he shimmied up the tree. I grabbed him by the back of the jumpsuit and yanked him up onto the branch with me.

"You okay?" I asked, brushing my hair out of my face.

"Are you?"

"I've been stuck in a tree all day, so I've been better," I said with a small laugh. "Why aren't you back at camp?"

"Missed you too much." It could've been the dark, but there was a sparkle in his eye that I'd never seen before. "I don't think I can sleep without you watching over me."

"That's sweet but," I glanced down at the circling wolves, reinvigorated with the scent of new blood, "now what?"

"We could stay here. It's a nice night, the company is great..."

"If you count the fifteen bloodthirsty animals, sure." I surveyed him, curious and a bit nervous about this new attitude of his. "What's gotten into you? Are you still concussed?"

He simply grinned. "So after all we've been through, you're going to let a pack of wolves get you down?"

"G-Galian," I said, laughing in spite of myself. "I've been here for hours. Why didn't you just..."

He glanced down. A wolf tentatively stepped forward and sniffed the stick. A piece of ember fell off and burned him, sending him yelping back to the rest of the pack. Even though it was dark, I could still make out fifteen bodies.

"How are we going to get rid of them?" I asked, leaning into the trunk of the tree.

"With this." Out of his pocket, he pulled a dark object: our flare gun. The only thing we had to signal we were alive on this island.

"Galian, you can't use that!" I gasped. "That's... We can't... What if we see another plane? We need to—"

"Theo, they aren't coming for us," he said. "Not after your ship blew up, and the lab and all this time. You know that as well as I do."

I was surprised, not because of his resolution, but because of how happy he sounded about it.

"Are you feeling all right?" I asked, leaning forward to press my hand against his head. To my heart-stopping shock, he took my hand gently and pressed a kiss to the palm.

"Yup."

I swallowed hard, now very much convinced he'd suffered serious head trauma, especially as he pulled me toward him.

The limb cracked beneath us and I looked into his wide eyes. Before either of us could react, it gave way and we crashed to the ground.

GALIAN

We tumbled to the ground, falling in a heap of human and tree limbs. The initial sound had scared off the wolves for a moment, but once the dust settled, they crept closer.

Theo wrapped her fingers around mine and whispered, "Galian, where is the gun?"

I fumbled for it, but it had disappeared in our fall. "I—I don't know..."

"Galian." She whimpered, sliding closer to me.

I wrapped my arm around her and pulled her close. "It's okay," I said, wondering when I became the strong one.

"I know."

In one fluid movement, Theo's arm flew by my face and a deafening crack echoed in the clearing.

I cried out and covered my ears, which were ringing. But when I lifted my head, the clearing was empty.

Theo trembled next to me, her hand still raised in the air with the now-useless flare gun in her hand and her eyes staring ahead like she'd just done something horrible.

"You okay?" I asked, rubbing my ears.

She nodded, but more out of habit than because she was listening. I gently took the flare gun and tossed it into the bushes, covering her cold, clammy hands with mine.

"What is it?"

"That was our last flare."

I cocked my head to the side. "Yeah. I know. What about it?"

"How are you going to get home?" she blurted and I was surprised that her first thought after nearly being wolf-food was getting me home. "How are you going to get back and make a difference in your country?"

"I... what?" It was rare to see her this affected.

"You have to go back," she said, glancing around and on the verge of tears. She was obviously still in shock, but there was something else. "You can't stay here forever. You need to go home, to live a good, long, happy life..."

I stood in front of her now, amused and in love with all that she was in this moment. "What if I'm happy living here with you?"

Her eyes flashed, and she retracted as if I'd struck her. For a brief moment I was afraid I had crossed the line, that she was going to turn and run away from me as fast as she could.

But I knew if I didn't kiss her right then, I'd regret it for the rest of my life.

FIFTEEN

THEO

Galian kissed me.

Right where we'd nearly been dinner for fifteen hungry wolves.

It was full lipped and glorious, and proof that he was every bit as experienced in wooing women as I'd read. Then it was more than a kiss, it was heaven that took my breath away.

He grasped the side of my face, holding me close to him, and gently opened my mouth with his tongue. He was definitely better at this than I was, and I let him take charge, ferociously, hungrily, mesmerizingly kissing me and I never wanted him to stop.

But he did, pulling away and staring into my eyes so desperately that I thought I might melt.

"What?" I whispered.

"I'm waiting for you to slap me."

Laughter burst from me. "Why would I slap you?"

It was his turn to look bewildered. "Because you... I..."

I grabbed his face and pressed my lips to his, not nearly as passionately as he'd assaulted mine, but enough to show him how I felt.

He moaned softly and pulled me closer, tasting and teasing me with his tongue before stopping suddenly.

"We should probably head back to camp." He grinned. "You know, in case the wolves come back."

"Good idea." I had no thoughts of my own in that moment, still reeling from our kiss.

"Shall I carry you?" he asked, that impish smile returning. "Seems like you liked it a lot."

My mouth fell open, and I was grateful for the darkness to hide my blushing face.

He leaned forward and kissed me again, whispering, "I plan to make you make that sound again."

I swallowed, but a giddy smile broke out on my face. I hopped onto his back and he nearly sprinted back to the cave. I licked my lips, tasting his kiss and daydreaming about what he planned to do once we returned there.

Our fire was low when we arrived home, with me still on his back, Galian tossed three branches into the center. He nearly tossed me onto the mattress, before crawling on top of me and pressing my hands into the mattress as he covered my mouth. I moaned in response as his hand moved to my chest, slowly and deliciously unzipping my jumpsuit.

He suddenly stopped.

"What am I doing? I've seen you naked before." He nearly ripped off the zipper of my jumpsuit, then took his off with equal ferocity, his eyes traveling the length of my naked body the whole time. My mind returned to me and I tensed, realizing what we were about to do.

"What's wrong?" he asked, sensing my nerves and immediately

looking to my broken leg. "Did I hurt you or—"

"No, it's just...I don't know," I said, unable to look at him. "I just... My legs are...hairy..." I actually didn't care, but I didn't want to tell him I'd never done this before. For all my talk about not caring about nudity, I was actually quite nervous.

"Well, there's such an abundance of razors and showers on this island, I'll never forgive you for not shaving," he teased me, before running his fingers down my thighs and then back up, and then disappearing between my legs.

Immediately, I forgot about my nerves as new and exhilarating sensations rolled up from where he touched me. His mouth covered mine as I clutched at him, writhing as he toyed with me, then slipped inside. Every inch of me was on fire, until the moment I couldn't take anymore. I closed my eyes and cried out, the waves of pleasures making me dizzy as I sank back down to the cold ground. I grinned at him; the son of a bitch looked so smug.

"Proud of yourself, are you?" I asked, unable to keep the breathlessness out of my voice.

"I thought you'd be harder to get off, to be honest. That was easy."

"Oh?" I said, remembering that he was an expert and, other than some private moments in my bunk, I was not.

He ran his hands down my hips, across my breasts, exploring my body while I came back down. He was gentle now, patient, placing kisses on my skin as I considered if I should tell him that I was a virgin. I was terrified of his response. He was the playboy prince, he'd been with tons of women, and what was he going to think of me?

"Wow," he said, his hand sliding back between my legs. "You feel amazing." My nervousness grew as he joined me on the floor. I couldn't take my eyes off of him, now fully erect, he was a lot to take in.

"Wait..." I whispered, stopping him before he entered me.

"What?"

"I've never...done this before." I looked away from him.

He took me by the chin and stared into my eyes. "Do you want to stop?" The tone in his voice eased my nerves. He hovered above me, tense and hesitant. And I knew that if I had asked him to stop, he would have. Because he was Galian, and that was why I loved him.

I shook my head with a small smile, less afraid than I had been. "I just wanted you to know."

He kissed me sweetly, his entire demeanor changing. His hands slid through mine and he slowly, deliberately, carefully entered me with a tenderness that overwhelmed me. It was tight and a little painful, and I'd hoped that my discomfort didn't show on my face.

"Okay?" he whispered in my ear. I pressed my lips to his in answer. "We'll go slow," he said, before adding with a playful nip of my shoulder. "For now."

We moved together, Galian taking his time until I felt more comfortable, and I simply enjoyed the new sensations. He'd said that it was better than flying, and I confess, the feeling of us joined together was incredible.

I looked up at him, and he kissed me again, something I swore I would never grow tired of.

"Are you all right?" he asked, pausing.

"Yes," I said.

"Are you sure?" he pressed, sliding deeper into me as if to prove a point. I couldn't help the moan that burst forth. He grinned and repeated the motion, and I tried my hardest to glare at him. But all I could do was smile like a moron. His deep thrusts grew quicker and more frenzied. He moaned as I had, and I wrapped my legs around his waist, pulling him closer as he squeezed my hands harder.

He came with a guttural sound that was very un-prince-like and quite possibly the sexiest thing I'd ever heard. He hung his head for a moment, collecting himself as he took gulping breaths. He shook his head and rolled off me, lying on his back.

"G—" Before I could say anything, he grabbed my arm and tucked me under his shoulder, pressing me tight to him and kissing my forehead. I felt safe there, and laid my head on his chest, amused by the rapid heartbeat under my cheek.

GALIAN

I could feel her heart pounding against my bare chest, and I held her tight to me. It felt right to have her there; she was perfect, exactly as she was. I wanted her again, but at that moment, it was all I could do just to hold her. I couldn't remember the last time I'd had sex, and the release after so much tension was... indescribable.

"Was that okay?" she asked me.

I looked at the top of the cave and tried to understand her words in my still addled brain. "Okay?"

"I mean..." she said, trying to get up, but I held her tight to me.

I placed another reassuring kiss on her forehead. "It was amazing," I said, and she relaxed in my arms. "You were amazing."

She settled her cheek against me and ran her finger down the center of my chest, sending chills down my spine. I turned my head to watch her, and noticed the concern still on her face.

"Theo," I said, rubbing her back. "It was amazing—"

"What are we going to do?" she whispered, cutting me off.

"About what?"

"Galian." My name on her tongue still made my heart race, especially when she lifted her eyes to look at me. "This...won't ever work."

"I think it worked just fine."

She gave me the tired look that I'd become so used to. God, I was so in love with this woman. "You know what I mean. If we ever get rescued—"

"Unlikely."

She snorted. "In the unlikely event that we get rescued, you're the *prince*."

"I'm also a human being. Not everything I do is dictated by someone else. Isn't that what you said?"

"Galian..." She hung her head.

"Look at me," I said, sitting up and cupping her cheek in my hand. "*When* the Kylaen forces come for us—for *us*," I emphasized, before she could respond, "you're coming back with me."

"But—"

"I love you, Theo," I replied and I watched her eyes widen. "I love you and I want you to come home with me."

She stared back at me with those beautiful dark eyes. In them, I could see the years of abuse, of fear, of living every day as if it were her last. She was Raven by birth, but they'd never loved her the way a country should love its child. They'd put her to work, enslaved her to a fighting force caught in a losing battle.

I wanted to show her what a country *could* be, how well she could be treated. I wanted to give her every opportunity that damn country never gave her. I wanted to protect her in the giant walls of Norose, where no harm could ever come to her.

And both our countries could just deal with it.

I kissed her fingers, realizing she hadn't answered. "So how about it? If we get rescued, will you come with me?"

THEO

He was nervous, and that made his question that much more honest. This man, this Kylaen royal—no, the man who'd saved my life time and time again, who had become my closest friend—he loved me. I could see it in his eyes, too. He had fallen for me as deeply and fully as I had for him.

He wanted me to come live with him in the glittering palace at Norose. He believed everything would work out for the best—as he always did. And I wanted to believe he was right. I wanted to believe it with every fiber of my being.

But if by some miracle we were rescued *and* they didn't kill me on the spot, there was no way we could ever be together. The idea was laughable.

I allowed myself to hope we'd never be found, but I dismissed it quickly. I wanted Galian to go home. I wanted it more than I wanted to be with him. Because he was a good person who deserved to live a long, full life of helping people. And I knew he could make a difference in his country if he believed he could. But he wouldn't leave without me.

I looked up into his eyes, those Kylaen eyes I'd somehow begun to love, just as I'd somehow begun to love the man who owned them. We'd beaten the odds and survived this long on an island that was determined to kill us. And we wouldn't have gotten this far if we weren't meant for something greater.

So I let myself believe.

"Yes," I whispered, closing my eyes to the sensation of the word already on the tip of my tongue. "I will go with you, *amichai*."

His face exploded in a grin as he pushed me down, ready to show me again just how much he loved me.

GALIAN

I was smiling before I even woke up. I felt her breath on my neck, her fingers resting on my chest, the warm body underneath the blanket with me. I ran my fingers down her bare back, all the way to her shapely, if not thin, butt and back up (and then down again, just for one final squeeze). I had known her body before, but now I was intimately familiar with it. I wanted to learn more, but hunger pains had awoken me.

I gently pushed Theo's hands off my chest and covered her in the blanket before I dressed myself. I wasn't quite finished with her yet, but I was hungry and I wanted to surprise her with some breakfast.

Preferably fish. No, I hadn't forgotten about that.

I leaned down to kiss her underneath her ear. "Morning."

She moaned softly, fluttering her eyes.

"I'll be back in a bit, okay?"

"Mmkay *amichai*," she whispered, rolling over and going back to sleep.

I climbed out of our cave and found my fishing pole. Carrying it to the beach, I flung the end of the pole into the water and waited for a moment. But Theo had been right; there weren't that many fish this far in. I decided to head back to the original camp, as there was more twine I could add to my line and maybe try to get the line out farther.

After an hour's walk back to camp, memories of the night before entertaining me, Theo's mangled ship greeted me. I had to laugh at how far she and I had come from that first day. She was a distrustful and severely injured feral cat, and me a helpless and naive princeling. Now, she was my Theo and I was her *amichai*.

I poked around the camp, thinking about the sound of the foreign word on her tongue. She had said the word was to be used only when felt deeply, like an involuntary response. Based on the number of times she used it the night before (I grinned stupidly), I'd have to agree.

"Ay-mi-kay," I tried. If I felt the way she did, could I pull off the pronunciation? It still sounded clumsy to me, so I kept practicing it.

"Ay-may-kay."

"No, aaaaaah-may-chai? No, that's not it."

"Ah-meh-chai."

"Ah—"

My voice died in my throat and my jaw fell open in shock.

"Your Highness!"

Sixteen

Theo

Galian was gone when I woke, but he'd left the blanket wrapped around me. Without him next to me, I was quite chilled, so I pulled on my jumpsuit, wondering how long I was going to be wearing it before Galian had it off again.

I giggled and it echoed off the walls of the cave, the same way our moans and frantic breathing had. I had to give him credit; sex was as good, if not better, than flying. But it wasn't just the way his fingers moved or his lips tasted, it was the way he looked at me. The way he smiled. I finally knew what it was to be loved by someone, and it was pretty damned incredible.

I wondered where he'd run off to, my princeling—no, my *amichai*. The word, even in my mind, was warm and comforting, and I sighed, reveling in the moment and this feeling. But even in my euphoria, I knew that once we got off this island, everything would disappear in an instant. Still, we'd been there for weeks, and there had been no sign of anyone. So perhaps what we were meant for was to live out our days on our island. Dashing away from wolves and making love by the fire.

I stretched, and a small squeak escaped my lips. That sounded like a pretty decent life to me.

I glanced at the cave ceiling, considering the problems that would arise if we continued to have unprotected sex. But like showers and razors, prophylactics weren't readily available. Yet another problem I could consider another day.

For the moment, I relived the long night together with a smile on my face. Now that this barrier was broken between us, now that everything was out in the open, this island was paradise. We could be together. We could love each other freely.

I rolled over and glanced out the cave. I bit my lip in giddy excitement, aching to see my *amichai* again. I imagined his arms pulling me close and his lips on my forehead. I stood and sauntered out of the cave lazily, daydreaming about him as I made my way over to the fire pit. Perhaps he was out catching breakfast.

I smiled to myself, thinking about our life together on the island. Everything was absolutely perfect.

"Hands on your head!"

GALIAN

I stood in the clearing, mouth agape. There was a person—a real, live person who was not myself or Theo on the island. Was I dreaming?

I blinked and rubbed my eyes, wondering if I was dreaming. I felt the heels of my hands in my eye sockets, so I couldn't have been.

"S-sire, is it really you?"

The voice was familiar, but I couldn't quite place the face. The stripes on the uniform meant something, but it had been so long since...

"Martin?" I gasped. The name came from some life long ago—a young two-striper who'd been assigned to protect me.

At once, realization washed over me.

They'd found me.

"Martin!" My face exploded in a smile as I rushed over to him, grasping him by the shoulder. I heard myself laughing. They'd found me. They hadn't left me. I was saved. Everything was going to be all right.

"Sire, it is...*very* good to see you," Martin said, grasping my arms as I did his. "We thought you were dead."

I couldn't help but laugh again. "I thought I was dead, too!"

Martin shared my excitement, glancing around the camp. "With all due respect, I thought I was going to find your remains here. How did you survive?"

My smile grew, thinking of Theo. I was going to make good on my promise. I couldn't wait to get her back to Norose and pamper the ever-loving *shit* out of her. I couldn't wait to see her in a dress. Preferably white.

After all, I wasn't bringing a Raven girl back to Norose just to date her.

"Sire?" Martin prompted me.

"It's a long story." I ran my hands through my hair. Far from the short military crop that Martin wore, my hair hung shaggy around my ears, my beard was thick and curly. "How long has it been?"

"Sire, you've been missing for two months," Martin replied. My breath left my chest. Two whole months? Time had flown, it seemed, and yet it also seemed as though I'd been there a lifetime. I tried to piece together the days and weeks in my mind and found I couldn't. Everything was a blur of rabbits and water and Theo.

"How did you find me? What's going on back in Kylae?"

Martin opened his mouth to speak then closed it, considering his words.

"Speak freely, Martin," I said, my mood darkening immediately. "His Royal Asshole-ness can't hear you. Trust me on that."

"Sire, I'm not sure...in your condition."

I snorted. "I don't have a condition, trust me. So everyone thinks that I'm dead?"

"We... There's already been a funeral procession," he said quietly. "We buried an empty casket."

I clicked my tongue against my teeth. "How long after?"

"Three days."

"Son of a bitch," I swore, turning to face the forest. "I knew it."

"But your mother...she wasn't convinced," Martin said. "Especially when several trading vessels reported seeing smoke in the northern islands. And...well, we received a note from Herin's northern radar station that they'd picked up some odd traffic."

I shook my head, anger seething inside me. All those times that I'd expected someone to come, those signs *had been* seen. Seen and ignored. "Let me guess. There was suddenly a need for every available resource for the war?"

Martin nodded. "Your mother asked me and Kader to look. It took us some time to pinpoint exactly where... I'm so sorry it took us this long—"

I quieted him by placing my hand on his shoulder. "Martin, you came right on time. Trust me on that." Had they come a day earlier, Theo and I would never have confessed our love, or spent a very pleasurable night in each other's company.

I clapped Martin on the arm. "Thank you for coming for me. Thank you for not giving up on me. You have no idea how good it is to see you." I looked at the ground as I became emotional. I probably had every right to be, but I didn't want to show it just yet. Later, I might cry like a baby in the comfort of my own home.

Home. I was going home.

"It was Kader, mostly," Martin's voice saved me from blubbering. "He's the one who was able to get passage out of Kylae to get here. He wouldn't rest until you were back home."

I furrowed my brow. "And here I thought he didn't like me very much."

"Pardon my frankness, but he doesn't," Martin said. I couldn't help but smile; his loyalty and deference extended only to my father, it seemed. "But he also didn't think it was right of your father to leave your body behind. He wanted to bring you home for your mother."

"Yeah, imagine the shock when he finds me living and breathing." I chuckled. "Where is that bald bastard anyway?"

"We split up about an hour ago."

"I..." My eyes widened. "We have to get back to my cave."

Before Kader found Theo.

THEO

The words didn't register, but the pain of being slammed into the ground did. I cried out from surprise and shock.

"Who are you?" I screamed. We hadn't seen another person on the island, and we had canvassed every single inch of it together. A million possibilities crossed my mind until I saw the shade of his uniform.

Kylaen.

They'd found us.

It was over. Our perfect paradise was gone in one fell swoop. There wasn't time for tears or anger, because I had a gun to my head, and if I didn't think quickly, I'd be looking at my brains on the ground.

"Get up, Raven *scum*," the man hissed at me, pulling me off the ground and pointing the barrel of his gun at my face. He was bald and tall, and from the snarl on his face, he wasn't one to be tangled with. *"Where is the prince?"*

"I... He's here... I...." I gasped, praying Galian would appear in the clearing. At this point, only he could save me.

"Where is he?"

"I promise, he's fine," I yelled in panic. I'd grown fond of one Kylaen, but I still thought the rest of them were a bunch of trigger-happy idiots. And I didn't like the half-crazed way this bald one was threatening me. "Just... please put the gun down. He just walked away for a minute. I'm sure—"

The gun pressed harder into my skull.

"Shut your filthy mouth." He threw me on the ground, and I stared up at him and the barrel, not making any sudden moves. He eyed the uniform I wore —the old Kylaen uniform we'd found in the radar station. "What are you wearing?"

"I found it here," I whispered.

His eyes narrowed. "I'll ask you again. *Where is the prince?*"

"I promise you," I winced as he cocked the gun, "I swear on my life that he's here. Galian is—"

"*Do not call him by his first name!*"

I shrank down again, averting my eyes. "The *prince* is here. I swear on my life that he is unharmed. He's healthy. He is... he's fine, I swear it."

"And why should I take your word for it?"

"Because..." I trailed off, almost telling this soldier that I loved Galian. But he'd probably kill me for saying such a thing. "Because it's the truth?"

"You Ravens are lying pieces of *shit*—"

"Kader. *Kader!*" My heart lifted to the skies as Galian ran into the clearing with another soldier behind him. I was saved, for the moment, at least. Although I knew everything was going to be much more difficult. The world which we'd kept at bay, the war which we'd set aside in favor of our love, it all was crashing back in. And there was nothing either of us could do to stop it.

The last thing I saw was the butt of the gun before everything went dark.

GALIAN

"*What the hell?*" I screamed as Theo slumped to the ground. I rushed past Kader, gently lifting her head, and touching the knot where

Kader's gun had knocked her out.

"Your Highness!" Kader sounded surprised, but I didn't care if he was surprised to see me alive or to see me caring for a Raven soldier. Saving me or not, he had no right to hurt Theo.

"That was unnecessary," I snapped, sliding my arms under her and picking her up. Her head fell against my chest limply. I'd get a better look at her when we got off this island, but for now, it was enough to keep her away from Kader until I could explain things.

"S-sire." Kader stepped forward. "Sire, we all thought you were dead."

"Well, I'm not, so can we get out of here, please?" I said, adjusting Theo in my arms. "I would really like a shower."

"Who is she?" Martin asked.

"She shot me down. Her name is Theo. She's coming with us."

Kader and Martin shared a look of surprise.

"S... What?" Kader said, blinking in confusion.

"She shot me down," I repeated, slower. "We're... She's coming with us. I promised her."

Kader cleared his throat. "That's all well and good, but in case you forgot, we're at *war* with her people. I don't think your father—"

"I could give a shit what he thinks," I snapped. "The dickhead left me on an island to die."

Kader glared at Martin, who withered. "He couldn't spare—"

"Save it. I know my father well enough to know he'd have rather you'd found a skeleton," I said. "But thanks to Theo here, I survived."

"We can't take her," Kader said.

I needed to make them understand. "Well, I'm sure it comes as no surprise that I had absolutely no idea how to fend for myself out here," I said, unashamed to admit my deficiencies in front of those who already knew them. "Theo's the reason I'm still alive." *And I'm the reason she's still alive*, I added silently, but I didn't want them to know that just yet. "I would have starved to death or died from dehydration without her. I...I love her." I straightened my shoulders, wondering why it was much scarier to admit my feelings to Kader and Martin than to the woman herself.

"Be that as it may," Kader said, more gently than I thought I'd ever heard him speak to me. "She's a sworn enemy of the crown."

"Then so am I."

Kader's fists balled in frustration and I half-expected him to deck me.

"Sire." Martin had decided to try, it seemed. "Let's all..." He glanced at Kader then back at me. "All of us go back to Norose. Get you and... your friend to a hospital."

I nodded to Martin and ignored Kader's angry look. They would have to pry me off the island if Theo didn't come with me. And I think Martin knew that.

"Let's go."

We marched quietly back to our original camp, passing by her deformed metal ship. Martin asked me how we'd ate, and I told him about Theo's rabbit traps and how we'd found an abandoned radar station on the other side of the island. That elicited a curious look from Kader, but he said nothing.

We continued our parade onto the nearby beach where my ship had landed two months ago. Further along the shoreline, I spotted a small plane with vertical take-off capabilities—the only way anyone would be able to land on the island. It told me that not only did they know I was on the island, but they'd also spent a few days planning the best way to retrieve me. When they got used to the idea that Theo was a part of my life, I'd thank them properly. With tears and free-flowing alcohol, most likely.

I stopped in the middle of the beach, mouth watering. Beer. Food. Food I didn't have to kill first. Dessert. Chicken. Lemon pie. Beer. Shower. Underwear. A toothbrush.

Clearing my throat, I adjusted Theo once more and followed my two rescuers onto their ship. The vessel was larger than the one I'd flown, this one had an area for cargo and was lined with jump seats along the edge. I stopped when I saw the wooden box in the center of the plane. My supposed coffin.

"Really, guys?" I asked, kicking it.

"Be careful or I'll bring you back in it anyway." Kader grunted, brushing past me to sit in the captain's seat. "Nobody knows you're alive."

I considered this and shut my mouth. I settled Theo into one of the seats and strapped her in tight. I placed a gentle hand on her cheek, wishing she would wake up so I could explain what was going on. But she continued to sleep soundly, though the welt on her head was growing.

"Sire, we're ready to take off." Martin's voice was quiet, but firm.

I settled in the seat next to Theo, strapping myself in. As the ship rumbled to life, the realization washed over me that I was leaving the island.

I was going home.

The feeling flooded through me and I found it hard to breathe for a moment. This nightmare was finally over. I had survived.

I glanced at the girl next to me and smiled. We had survived.

She had saved me, I had saved her. And through our struggle, we'd found something even better.

I watched the sandy beach and forest disappear. The gray ocean waves that lapped against the shore. As we rose higher, I saw the crater where the laboratory had been. For as much as it had given us, I felt a duty to ask some serious questions about what happened there. My father, at least, owed me an explanation for why he continued to pretend like Mael wasn't killing people.

But as the ship gained altitude, I decided those problems would be addressed later, after I'd had a shower and a full meal. And maybe after a long nap with Theo in my arms.

Kader pressed the ship forward, toward Norose and Kylae and all of the real-world problems I was sure would come roaring in our direction as soon as we landed. But I glanced back at the small dot of land rapidly disappearing against a sea of blue, and I knew that whatever they threw at us, we could handle together.

"We're going home, Theo."

SEVENTEEN

GALIAN

Kader landed the ship in the small military airfield near the capital city, the very same one that I had taken off from two months before. My survival had not been broadcast, it seemed, because there was no greeting party or tabloid photographers waiting and Kader, Martin, Theo (still asleep), and I piled into what I assumed was Kader's personal car. There was barely any leg room for me, but Theo and I managed.

"You stink," Kader grunted from the front seat after we'd been driving for a while.

"It's been a while since I've showered," I replied, glancing over at Theo, curled up under my arm. "You know, we were a little focused on trying not to starve to death," I continued, brushing the hair off her face. "If I'd known you guys were coming to get me, I'd have jumped into the Madion Sea."

Martin snorted and the corners of Kader's mouth turned upward.

"Besides, Theo didn't mind."

"I'll bet she didn't," Kader muttered.

I was about to snap at him when we crossed a hill, and the city of my birth grew larger on the horizon. I pressed my face to the car window, taking in every single detail. I'd never considered Norose mine or held any love for it when I was growing up, but now...now it was the most beautiful thing I'd ever seen.

I glanced at Theo—except for her, of course.

We passed the long strip of statues that marked the main drag of the city to the castle. An abundance of black ribbons hung from the street lamps.

"The king declared a period of mourning to last ninety days," Martin said, when I asked.

"Ninety, wow," I said, sitting back. "That's thirty more than Dig got. I guess I should be touched that he thought so highly of me."

"There was also an uptick in enlistments," Kader said. "More young men wanting to avenge your death."

"Maybe I'll just stay dead then. Let them all kill each other." I glanced down at Theo, then shook my head. Running away was something the old Galian would've done. Now I had a chance to be better.

When Kader turned down the long causeway to the Royal Kylaen Hospital, a rush of glee washed over me. The big, beautiful white building gleamed in the late afternoon sun, seven stories' worth of windows reflecting the sun and the Madion Sea.

Kader, not having the royal car, pulled into the emergency room entrance. I opened the car door and stepped out, almost ready for the rush of people that normally accompanied my arrival. But since I was still dead, there was nothing. Two young nurses caught a glimpse of me—I recognized one who'd made eyes at me when I was a resident.

But they took one look at my bedraggled clothes and disgusting beard and scurried away.

"Galian."

Dr. Maitland's face was as I'd remembered it—his cheeks still round, the liver spots still adorning his bald head. But his eyes reflected emotion I'd never seen in them.

"Dr. Maitland, it's—" I meant to shake his hand, but he pulled me into a hug so tight it was hard to breathe.

"Son, I thought we'd lost you," he said, stepping back. "It's...well, it's *damned* fine to see you."

I grinned at him and reached into the car to pull out Theo.

"Who is that?"

"This is Theo," I said, wishing she'd just *wake up* already. She was missing too much excitement. I couldn't wait for her to meet Maitland. "She crashed on the island with me. Shot me down, actually."

"Galian, is she...Raven?"

I nodded and adjusted her in my arms. "She has an injury on her left leg I want you to take look at. She can't walk on it very well. I think the gash on her other leg has healed, but—"

"Galian," Dr. Maitland said, cutting me off. "She is fine. How about you? That's a nasty bruise on your forehead."

"My forehead?" My fall seemed a lifetime ago, but it had only been a day or two since I'd woken up. "Malnourished, dehydrated, maybe a small concussion."

"You didn't sustain any injuries in the crash? No hypothermia?"

"I parachuted out," I said. "What's the story my father's been telling everyone?"

His old eyes grew sad and solemn. "You crashed in the ocean.

Fighting off ten planes."

"It was one, and she kicked my ass," I said, glancing down at her with pride. "But her ship exploded, and that's how she landed there too. She was in rough shape—bleeding out."

"And you saved her life?"

"Of course I did," I said, blushing at the open pride Dr. Maitland displayed. "It was the right thing to do. And now we're home."

Maitland's brows knitted together, and he placed a gentle hand on my arm. "*You* are home. She, however, is now in an enemy country."

I frowned. "She's my guest here. Are you telling me you won't care for her?"

"I will tend to her," Maitland said, sharing a glance with Kader, "but you should tread very carefully. Consider the consequences of what you've done—"

"I have," I snapped. Did everyone think I was a moron?

"Very well," Maitland said with a small nod. "Let's take her to the basement so no one sees either of you. I'm sure you'd like some time to gather yourself before the world knows you're really alive."

The basement rooms were chilly, and I realized I'd forgotten how good air conditioning felt. Many of our charity cases were treated in the basement, so it didn't look too odd for a bedraggled man to be carrying a dark-skinned girl down there. Luckily for the two of us, the staffing was already light and easily dismissed by Dr. Maitland. We placed Theo in the last room at the end of the hall where we could assess her without attracting too much attention.

"I don't think it's a fracture," Maitland said, pressing against the skin on her leg. It was still blotchy. "Perhaps hairline if she was able to walk on it."

"She'd gotten better over the past few weeks," I said. "Can you check her other leg? She had a pretty bad laceration that she sustained in the crash."

Maitland replaced the blanket over her leg and placed his hand on the bed, sighing deeply. "Sire, what are you going to tell your father?"

"I haven't quite gotten that far yet," I said, running a hand over my beard.

My mother's voice drew my attention. She stood in the doorway, her face whiter than I'd ever seen it, and her hands clamped over her mouth as if holding in a scream. Her hair, normally combed and neat and curled in public, was stringy and hanging around her face as if she no longer cared how she looked. Even her clothes, a long-sleeved t-shirt and dark pants, were ones I'd never seen her wearing outside her personal wing of the castle.

"Mom," I said, grinning.

She stepped into the room slowly at first, before rushing towards me and wrapping me in a neck-breaking hug. "I thought you were dead," she whispered, stepping back a bit to look at my face. "Galian, you're... Oh, my baby boy!"

I awkwardly patted her on the shoulder as she cried into mine. "It's okay, Mom," I said, smiling to Maitland who took his cue to give us some privacy. "I'm fine, really."

"Mom, you're hurting him."

My head bobbled at the sound of Rhys's voice. I grinned at him, drinking in the sight of his mocking eyes and that idiotic goatee he refused to shave. He, at least, looked like himself, with his crisp green collared shirt and slacks. The only thing that seemed different was the genuine relief shining in his eyes. He clapped my shoulder, as that was all he could get from my mother.

I did not, however, see my father. For that, I was grateful.

My mom continued to check my face, fussing over every scratch and bruise on it, commenting on my beard and the state of my clothes. "Gally, you're too thin," she said, pinching my arms.

Rhys' eyes lit up at the name. "Yeah, *Gally*, guess that's what happens when you're marooned on an island for two months." His amusement turned into an amazed smile. "I don't even know how you survived out there."

My attention turned to Theo, still peacefully sleeping in the bed next to me. "Her. She's the one who did most of the work. She taught me how to hunt and make a fire. I would've been dead if it weren't for her."

"And you also wouldn't have been on that island in the first place," Rhys said, cocking his head as he examined her from afar. "She's cute. Good thing you didn't land there with an ugly girl."

My anger flared, and my mother felt it.

"Rhys," she warned, in the voice she hadn't used since we were boys. My brother, nearly thirty, hadn't been spoken to like that in years and immediately clammed up. "She is a guest in our kingdom, and should be treated as such."

"Father is pissed you brought her here," Rhys said, folding his arms over his chest. "Thinks you should've shot her and thrown her body in the Madion Sea."

"If you *touch* her," I snarled, restrained only by my mother.

"No one is going to hurt her," she said. "After all, it appears we have her to thank for keeping you alive."

Rhys threw back his shoulders, like he had any say in the

matter. "Mom, it's tricky. She's Raven—"

"She's a human being, and her name is Theophilia Kallistrate," I snarled, letting my anger get the better of me. "She's nineteen years old, and she's an orphan. She's been a pilot since she was twelve, and all she wants is to be free. And..." My words caught in my throat. "And I love her."

"Gally, you've been through a lot," Mom said, patting my hair. "You need to rest. Dr. Maitland will take good care of... Theophilia." She hesitated at the name, but I knew she was trying. "Come home. Take a shower, get into some real clothes. Have a real meal. I promise, you'll be back before Theophilia wakes up. And we will figure out how to handle your father together."

I considered the oddness of having my mother speak about Theo, and I was suddenly very tired.

"I shall keep watch over her." Dr. Maitland stood behind us. "Go home, Galian. Get some rest and some food. I have a feeling you'll need both."

"C'mon," she said, looping her arm through mine. "And, Gally, you do need a shave."

THEO

I awoke to a white ceiling. My head was pounding, and the last thing I remembered was...

My eyes opened wider as I tried to move my hands, finding only a few inches of movement before the chains around my wrists stopped my movements. I moved my legs, ignoring the pain in my still-healing leg, and found them similarly bound by thick shackles. Instead of my Kylaen uniform, I now wore a clean, white hospital gown. But I was a captive, and they had spared no expense to ensure I remained that way.

He'd said we'd be together in Kylae, didn't he? So why was I chained up? My initial suspicions returned. They must have thought I was a high value prisoner of war. Or perhaps the Kylaen military was so deranged they wanted me whole before they destroyed me.

My thrashing must've alerted the medical staff, as an old man came scurrying in, wearing a white lab coat. He checked a panel on the wall, one measuring my heartbeat and blood pressure. He turned to adjust the drip on the bag of fluid connected to my arm.

"Where's Galian?" I asked, my voice no higher than a whisper.

"He's resting at the castle," the doctor replied, placing the tablet under his arm. "I'm a little concerned about the injury on your left calf, so I've scheduled an x-ray for the morning. You have a very mild concussion, and a bit of dehydration and malnourishment. But other than that, you are perfectly fine."

Fine? How was I supposed to be fine when I was in Kylae? Chained up, and Galian was no where to be found.

"Calm yourself, my dear," the old doctor said with a chuckle. "I promise you, Galian will be back as soon as he can. He asked me to look after you in his absence."

When I turned to look at him, I saw his badge and my heart beat faster. "Dr. Maitland," I breathed.

"Believe me, he didn't want to leave," he said with a kind smile, "but his mother was insistent that he eat something."

His mother. Galian's mother. The queen. The queen was here.

Was the king? Did he know? I suddenly missed Galian's presence even more. With him, at least, I might've had some protection. Without him, there was an entire country out to kill me.

"Am I a prisoner?" I asked, looking to the shackles on my hands and feet.

Maitland placed the tablet down and began unhooking my hands and feet. "Forgive me for the restraints, but I didn't think it wise to allow you to roam around the hospital until we'd had a chance to talk. To answer your question, no, you aren't a prisoner. In this hospital, we simply have patients. And you, my dear, are mine."

I pulled my hands to my chest and rubbed my wrists. "That's what Galian said when he saved my life." I snorted. "The first time."

"The story he tells is that you saved his," Dr. Maitland replied.

I couldn't help the smile that grew on my face, but I tried very hard to hide it. Maybe things wouldn't be as bad as I'd thought they would be. Maybe Galian and I could figure out a way to be together back in the real world.

Dr. Maitland patted me on my good leg. "I will bring Galian to you as soon as he arrives back here," he said, his eyes sparkling a little. "Which, if I know him, will be as soon as he can."

GALIAN

I flopped, buck-naked, into my bed, and let out a loud, satisfied sigh. My hair was still wet from the longest shower I'd ever taken, and I wanted to savor in this clean feeling for eons. I'd also shaved, though I might grow a bit of a short beard now that I knew I could. I'd ask Theo about it when I saw her at the hospital.

I sat up and flew out of bed. I had plenty of time to sleep in it when Theo was sleeping with me. She had surely woken up by now, and I'd hoped Dr. Maitland had explained everything to her. But knowing Theo, she wouldn't relax until I was by her side.

I stood and went to my expansive closet, finding a pair of boxers and enjoying how clean they felt. It was the best feeling in the world. I'd probably send someone to go pick out a new wardrobe for Theo. She may not like the Kylaen fashions, but at least I could find her something simple.

My mother leaned against the doorframe of my bedroom, her eyes lighting up when she saw me. We considered each other for a moment until she broke the silence.

"It's nice to see you there."

I laughed, running a hand through my wet hair. "It's nice to see you there, too, Mom."

Emotion cracked her face and her lip trembled. "I didn't believe that you were dead. I...I couldn't believe that you were dead."

I stood and walked over to her, the weeks of worry and grieving evident on her face. She hadn't given up on me. "Mom..."

"I will *never* forgive your father," she hissed, closing the door behind her. "Digory wanted to go to battle. But you? You were doing good things and—"

"Mom, it's okay," I said, placing my hand on her shoulder. "It was my choice to go. And I'm glad I went. Because I found Theo."

"Galian, you can't..." She trailed off. "She's... You can't be truly in love with her. I understand you two went through a lot but..."

I took a step back, shocked that my own mother would've

doubted my feelings for Theo. "It's more than that. She's... she's amazing. She's got this spirit, and her loyalty. I just...I can't explain it. I just know that I am in love with her. I don't have to justify it."

"I'm sorry," she said quickly. "And I can't wait to meet the girl that my little boy has fallen in love with. But..." She furrowed her brow and cupped my face. "Darling, you understand that if you walk out of that hospital with a Raven soldier on your arm, it's going to... cause problems."

"I don't care—"

"You have to care, Gally." She smiled sadly. "I'm so thrilled that you've found someone that you are this passionate about. But you have to know that this is going to be difficult for your people to accept. We are at *war* with—"

"Then let's stop the war," I said. "Stop bombing them. Done. War over."

"Gally, you know it's not that simple—"

"It *is* that simple, Mom. But His Royal Asshole-ness—"

"*Galian Neoptolemos Helmuth!*" Her shocked voice echoed in my room. "I understand that you've been gone, but if your father hears you—if *anyone* hears you speaking that way...I don't know if I can protect you from him. And if you can't protect yourself, how are you going to protect your Theo?"

I stopped before I retorted, knowing that my mother was right. I had become a little reckless with freedom, and I needed to remember that I was back in my father's kingdom, at his whim.

And yet, Theo had told me I had a choice. I needed to see her. She was always better at coming up with plans.

"And speaking of which, your father is expecting you in his study."

A drip of fear slid down my back. "Mom, I have to get back to the hospital. Theo needs me."

"It will take two minutes, I'm sure," she said with a bitterness I didn't miss. She and Rhys were glad to see me, but my father might not be so pleased. "Pop your head in and show him that you're alive. Then you can go to the hospital. Theo will be fine."

THEO

Dr. Maitland left me in a silent, chilly room, offering me the shower as long as I took care on my leg. I stood under the water forever, finally warm after so many weeks of frigid temperatures. I found a new hospital gown waiting for me on the bed, and I relished the clean feeling as I slipped back into bed. Before I knew it, I was back asleep.

I stirred when the door opened and Dr. Maitland appeared with a tray of food in his hand. The smell of it was mouthwatering. When he approached, I saw that his badge read *Chief of Medicine*. I didn't know much about hospitals, but I knew that bringing a patient food was probably not on his list of duties. Seeing how attentive he was, I could see where Galian had learned his bedside manner.

"Slowly, Theo," he said, placing it in front of me. "You need to eat slowly, else this won't stay down."

I nodded, taking the fork as if it were a foreign object and sticking it through the potatoes. I put the glorious creamy mixture in my mouth and closed my eyes, savoring it.

"I've never seen someone so pleased to eat hospital food," he said, sitting on the bed after checking my vitals.

"You've never had to kill a rabbit, I take it," I said.

"There were rabbits?"

I took another bite, slowly so he wouldn't fuss at me. "We had the luck of crashing on one of Kylae's secret testing laboratories. We found..." I trailed off, taking another bite. I didn't want to think about it while enjoying the most amazing canned vegetables I'd ever had in my life.

"I'm not aware of any Kylaen facilities up that way," Maitland said, sitting back. "These rabbits, how did you trap them?"

"First we dug a hole," I said. "Covered it with leaves and ate whatever we caught. I was able to build a cage after a few days."

"Why didn't you kill the prince?"

I nearly choked on the peas in my mouth. "I...what?"

"You could have killed the prince. That's what you were sent there to do, wasn't it?" he said. "You spent two months alone with him. Why didn't you kill him?"

My heartbeat quickened. At this point, I figured honesty was the best policy with him at this point. "I...thought about it, I won't lie. But at the time, I was injured and I couldn't have survived without him."

"And now?"

I half-smiled, realizing how stupid I was about to sound. "Now I love him."

"Why?" Maitland asked.

I shrugged. "Because he's Galian."

"That's not much of a reason," he said.

My eyes narrowed and I wondered when the princeling was going to return. Perhaps Maitland's kindness was just an act. Was this food poisoned? "I'm not sure why I'm being asked."

Maitland sighed and removed his glasses. "Because, my dear, you are a Raven captain in Kylae. There will be questions about why you're here, whether your intentions are truthful or if you were sent here as a spy."

"I just spent two *months* half-starved on a deserted island with him. Do you think—?"

"I know Galian," Maitland cut me off. "Probably as well, if not better, than you. And I know why you fell in love with him. But if your intentions are questioned, you need to have a better response than true love."

I sighed and looked down at the tray, suddenly not hungry. "For a moment, Galian had me believing everything would just...magically work itself out. I guess that's just Galian, huh? Stupid princeling has never had to worry about a thing in his life."

Maitland chuckled softly and patted my hand. "Galian's optimism is infectious, I know. When he was a resident here, nothing ever seemed to bother him. He took every challenge with an unyielding belief that everything would work out for the best."

In spite of all my worry, I grinned. "He's so stupid. Stupid, and beautiful and kind. Sometimes I wish I could see life like he does."

"We all can use a bit of Galian's optimism," Maitland said. "We just have to—"

A ruckus down the hall drew his attention. Brows knitted together, he walked to the closed door only seconds before it burst open, and the room was filled with Kylaen soldiers.

"What is the meaning of this?" Maitland bellowed, taking up

more room than his small frame would suggest.

"Move out of the way."

"She is a patient—"

I yelped when the soldier used the butt of his gun to knock Maitland away. He fell to the ground and lay there, eyes closed.

Rough hands yanked me out of the bed, spilling my platter of half-eaten food on the ground. Then there were five guns in my face.

"Get dressed." He thrust my dirty clothes from the island at me. I swallowed and turned to disrobe, but the head Kylaen pulled me to face him.

"Where I can *see* you."

The hospital gown fell to the floor, and I desperately wondered where the hell my *amichai* was...

EIGHTEEN

GALIAN

I paced in front of my father's study, much to the chagrin of his personal secretary and the two guards out front.

"I need to get in there," I said, again, to the secretary.

"Sire, he's in with his cabinet."

"And I've just come back from the dead!" I huffed.

It had been too long since I'd seen Theo, and I was worried she'd think I'd abandoned her. Three or four times in the past half-hour, I had considered turning and walking away. Ignoring an official demand from my father.

But my fear kept me in place. I was still a coward. Perhaps Theo could teach me how to be brave with my father.

I paused in front of the doors again and imagined her walking these castle halls with me. The refinement and pomp would sicken her when so many people lived in squalor. So we wouldn't live in the castle. Maybe we could find a little place somewhere secluded. Maybe we'd escape to another country and live out a quiet life away from everything.

I glanced at the clock again as another minute had ticked by.

"This is ridiculous," I said to the secretary.

"His Majesty is on his own schedule."

I made sure he saw the gigantic eye roll.

After an eternity, the doors opened, and my father and his cabinet members strolled out of the room, smelling of brandy and cigar smoke. I crossed my arms over my chest—this was more important than seeing his not-dead son?

Then again, he hadn't given me much thought after my plane disappeared, so why was I expecting anything more?

"Father." I announced my presence since the gaggle of old, bald men walked right by me.

One by one, they turned around. It took them a moment—although my face was shorn of my beard, my hair was long and dangling around my ears.

"My stars."

"It's..."

"He's alive!"

"Yes, yes."

My father, tall, imposing, his face devoid of my mother's worry and grief, pushed to the front of the crowd. Before he turned to face his advisors, he plastered a pained expression on his face and embraced me tightly. I stood stiffly, considering when the last time my father had *ever* embraced me.

He stood back from me, a warning look in his eye, and he turned to face his cabinet.

"We have been keeping it quiet, but my son has been found alive!"

They exploded into applause and my father bowed slightly, as if he could take credit for my survival. I withheld a grimace when his arm looped around my shoulders.

"We have been secretly searching for him for two months," he said. I was amazed at how easily he was able to lie. "His mother and I knew there was a chance that he'd survived, that he was still alive. But we dared not announce it, since the Ravens were so intent on killing him. I wouldn't be able to forgive myself if they'd found him before we did."

I didn't bother to mask my disbelief.

"Last night, we got a call from his personal bodyguard, who I'd tasked to search the northern islands in the Madion Sea." Another lie. "He said he had spotted wreckage from a plane on the beach, and this morning," my father squeezed me tightly against him, "*this morning* we found him!"

More applause from the cabinet members, who savored this story as deliciously as fine wine.

"With—" I started, but my father's voice overtook me.

"I had my doubts about my son, as you all are aware. But to survive, *alone,* for two months!"

My first thought was to ask him why he'd discussed me with his cabinet, but then I realized what he'd said. "I wasn't—"

"He learned to hunt, he learned to fend for himself. I couldn't be prouder. But I've always said that with just a little push, he could be the sort of prince Kylae has always deserved."

"Father," I hissed, ripping my arm out of his grasp.

"My poor boy has been through a lot," he said. "If you'll give us a moment to catch up, father-to-son..."

I didn't even wait for them to leave before turning on him. "What kind of bullshit is this? You know I wasn't alone—"

"As far as this story goes, boy, you *were*." My father, dropping his smarmy veneer, was back to the same jackass I knew. "As far as your companion...I've solved that problem for you."

My heart fell into my stomach. "What are you talking about?"

"You will sit for interviews, talk to the media," he continued, ignoring my question completely. "We will use this story to bolster support for the war. My son, the survivor!"

"*I wasn't alone*," I spat through gritted teeth. "What have you done?"

"Galian!" I heard a voice calling me from down the hall and saw Dr. Maitland rushing toward me.

My father patted me on the shoulder. "I told you, I took care of it." He paused to glance at my hair. "Tell your handler to schedule you a hair appointment. We can't have you walking around looking like that."

"Galian," Dr. Maitland said breathlessly. A purple bruise was growing on his left temple, and my anger multiplied. "Your father's soldiers came, and they took her. There was nothing I could do, nothing I could say." His face shone with anguish. "Galian, I'm sorry...she's gone."

"Where did they take her?" I asked, knowing and dreading the answer.

THEO

I was going to Mael.

They didn't have to tell me. They *didn't* tell me. They barely even looked at me once the dirty uniform was back on my body. Something about the way they'd leered at me made me want to take a bath in molten lava.

They covered my head and shoved me onto a metal bench, encircling my wrists and ankles with thick iron shackles. Then we rode. The bench was slippery, and more than once I slid into one of my captors when we went over a nasty bump. They shoved me off, spitting with anger that I'd dared touch them.

I closed my eyes since I couldn't see anyway, and let all the self-hating thoughts consume me. I shouldn't have been surprised to be in this position. I knew when Galian spoke of me returning with him that it would never work. I knew when we *crashed* that it would've been smarter for me to kill myself than wait for Kylaen forces to take me to their death camp.

I imagined the Raven slaves forced to endure the testing on the laboratory. I wondered how many of them killed themselves before the Kylaens killed them first.

For a moment, I tried to get angry at Galian for bringing me to his country, for putting me in danger. But I couldn't. He'd truly thought I would be safe with Dr. Maitland. Truly thought we could make this work. His naive optimism was one of the reasons I loved him so much.

But the shackles on my hands reminded me of the harsh reality.

I felt the car slow and forced myself to think about Galian. If I were to remain strong, to keep myself from falling apart from fear, I needed to focus on something else. I let my mind wander to the mornings when I woke up to see him standing over the fire. I pictured the way the sunlight bounced off his pale skin, remembered how it felt when he whispered my name. When he kissed me. The sound of him telling me he loved me.

"C'mon!" Hands roughly pulled me off of the bench and into the open. Through the hood still on my head, the noxious gas filled my nose. I remembered reading the laboratory file: two hundred times the ingested amount before it was fatal.

I tried hard not to breathe, but I couldn't help it.

The hood was ripped off, along with some of my hair, and I looked around at the building I had only seen in pictures. Large smokestacks billowed white smoke into the sky. Grimy windows lined the rusty old building. The fences were high and covered in barbed wire.

"Move it!"

They shoved me forward, and I stumbled, my still-broken leg protesting the extra weight. I walked normally on it as best I could, even though it screamed in pain.

Five other prisoners stood in line. Most of them had the pale Kylaen skin, but I spotted one man darker in color. I tried to catch his eyes, but they stared blankly ahead, as if already dead.

We stood in a courtyard for what felt like eons, and my leg began to hurt so badly it made me sick. Or perhaps the smell was starting to get to me. I tried to take shorter breaths, hoping I might inhale less of the poison.

Next to me, one of the lighter-skinned prisoners was muttering to himself. I saw him counting on his fingers in antsy anticipation.

I wanted to say something to him, wanted to tell him my trusty phrase about not making it this far just to die, but I couldn't bring myself to do it. This was truly the end for everyone who set foot in there. There was no way out.

"We're going to die," the man to my right whispered.

"Stay calm," I whispered back.

"We're going to die." He began to shuffle forward, his eyes wild and crazed.

A crack echoed in the courtyard, and I turned away so I wouldn't see him lying there on the ground. How much longer would I last before I lost my mind from fear?

A very real, palpable fear washed over me, one that I hadn't felt since my very first battle. My stomach was in my throat, but I swallowed hard. I refused to appear weak in front of these monsters.

Closing my eyes, I forced myself to remember how it felt when Galian kissed my hand in the tree. The look on his face when he said he loved me. I vowed I would keep his memory in the forefront of my mind until my dying breath.

"Well, well, look what we have here, a full-blooded Raven girl." His hand grabbed my face and forced me to face him. I couldn't see his face through a thick gas mask, but his eyes glittered.

I forced myself to think of the island, of cold nights in front of the fire. Watching Galian sleep, or pretend to sleep until he gave up and talked with me through the night.

"It's been a while since we've had a full Raven. They usually last a lot longer than the others here. Must be that slave blood in their system."

I imagined Galian's laughter, how it had felt when he'd come back into the camp after being away for a few hours.

"Send her into the pit with the rest of the dogs."

"*Amichai*," I whispered to myself as they pulled me forward, my foot kicking the body of the man at my feet.

GALIAN

I spotted Kader standing next to my car. I didn't remember walking up to him, but I sure remembered the feeling when my fist connected with his jaw.

"*You son of a bitch!*" I screamed.

"I was just doing what I was instructed," Kader said, rubbing his jaw.

My punch didn't even lay him out, so, furiously, I reared back to hit him again, but he grabbed my arm and spun me around, pinning my arm behind my back.

"Calm down, Galian," he said, sounding too normal for what he'd just done.

"You sentenced her to death," I spat out. "You... Why did you *tell* him?"

"Because it was the right thing to do," Kader said in my ear. "Are you going to try to hit me again?"

"I'm going to tear your fucking head off!"

Kader's grip tightened on my arm. "You aren't thinking clearly. Otherwise, why would you think bringing a Raven girl back with you was a smart idea?"

"Because I love her!" I bellowed.

"You may think that—"

That was too much. I kicked Kader in the shin, and he released me. I heaved for a moment, anger and exertion taking their toll.

"I am *completely* in control of my own emotions," I growled.

"Do you think I'm an idiot? Do you think I don't know that we've been at war with them? *She shot me down!*"

"Then how can you expect me to believe that you fell in love with her?" Kader said. "She was the only pussy on the island, I get it, but—"

"Don't you *ever* talk about her that way again. That girl, she *saved my life* more times than I can even *count*. I would be *dead* if it weren't for her! And you expect me to just send her off to her death because my *father* thought it was a better story to say that I survived all by myself?"

Kader said nothing.

"She is a human being," I said, amazed that I even had to say that. "She's not just a Raven any more than I'm just a Kylaen. She...she deserves more than this. She took care of me. And now she's going to die." My eyes narrowed. "I should've told you to leave us there."

"We couldn't do that," Kader said, rubbing his jaw. "You're too thin as it is. You wouldn't have survived—"

"I survived for two months with *her*," I said defiantly. "Fuck you for thinking otherwise."

Again, Kader said nothing and I stared north again. Where those bastards had taken my Theo.

"I'm going after her."

"That's ridiculous," Kader said. "You can't—"

"I'm the prince. I can do whatever I want." I gritted my teeth and brushed past him. "And I'm going to get my Theo back."

I slid into the front seat of Kader's car and searched for the keys. I hadn't driven a car since I was sixteen, swerving around a deserted airfield with my guard at the time, but I could probably remember the gist of it. I'd figured out how to skin a rabbit, I could figure this out.

Kader slid into the passenger seat next to me, as if he were going out for a leisurely drive. "Are you serious about going after her?"

"Give me the keys," I said. "I'm going to take down the front gate. I'll order them—"

"I might remind you that your father left you for dead for two months."

"So?"

"So if you went to his death camp, demanding that your girlfriend be released, he might have a problem with that," Kader said, putting his hands behind his head. "And you might find yourself in that prison with her."

"Then I'll just sneak her out."

Kader snorted. "You're as stealthy as a fighter jet."

I growled in frustration.

"Do you even have a plan to get her?" Kader asked lazily.

"I... what?" I blinked, expecting him to argue with me more.

"A plan, Sire," he asked, looking quite annoyed. "To rescue your Raven girl." He paused as I opened my mouth. "Your...Theo."

I closed my mouth, too shocked to respond.

"Are you truly serious about putting your life on the line? To put someone else before yourself and your own safety? Even if it means that you'll be known as a traitor to your country?" He looked at me, and I shrank from the intensity of his glare. "Because that's what'll happen if you set this girl free. You'll have to give up your princely life and your fancy parties and all the special treatment you receive."

"In case you forgot, I *had* none of that for two months," I retorted, but it lacked some of my previous fire.

"But now you have a chance to have it back, and then some.

You could have any girl in Kylae that you wanted. Dr. Maitland would welcome you back at the hospital. Life could return to normal. All you have to do is hand over the keys and go back to the palace and forget all about your girlfriend."

In response, I stuffed the keys into the ignition and turned the car on. "Fuck off. I'm getting my girl out of there."

"Fine," Kader said, reaching over to turn off the car. "But if we do this, we do it my way."

I whipped my head around. "I thought you said—"

"If your father finds out that I let you waltz into Mael, *I'll* be the one behind bars," Kader said, as if discussing the weather. "So if you're really going to do this—"

"I am."

"Then I guess I have to make sure you don't fuck it up. For my sake."

I stared at him as if I'd never seen him before. Kader had been gruff, but he'd never spoken so...plainly to me before. Perhaps my own newfound freedom had rubbed off on him.

"What do we do first?" I asked.

THEO

I was deposited in the center of the iron building, my shackles attached to a line of sickly looking prisoners. I tried my best to ignore the woman to my left, or the tumor growing out of her cheek. Her eyes were heavy-lidded as she shoveled the black material from one pile to another.

"*Shovel, bitch.*" The voice behind me was on my neck, and I picked up the shovel in front of me.

I was to move the black stones from the mountain next to me into my neighbor's pile, and then she to hers, and so on until it reached the burning fire pit in the center. I realized this was the source of the poison. I couldn't remember the name Galian had used—

Galian.

I forced myself to remember what he looked like, what he smelled like. The sound of his voice. I wanted to keep it in the forefront of my mind, just in case I dropped dead. I wanted him to be my last thought.

"*Shovel faster!*"

I sneered at a guard who was screaming at a boy as he cowered in fear. If my hands hadn't been shackled to the ground, I would've run over and snapped the guard's neck.

There were more than a few children in this wretched place. They were old enough to have been pilots, but rarely did I hear of a Raven pilot who'd been taken prisoner. They didn't look fully Raven either, with some having Kylaen blue eyes and lighter hair. But they shared the same, scared look that my young lieutenants did before we'd left for a mission.

I shifted my weight for a second onto my bad leg and then back onto my good one, which was aching from standing on it for so long. Galian used to get on me for using it too much.

I paused for a moment, reaffirming his presence in my mind.

"Don't *stop*." The breath was behind me again, and I continued working, my lungs burning with the disgusting gas that would eventually kill me.

NINETEEN

GALIAN

I remembered the first time I'd been to Mael. I was hungover as shit, but that didn't matter to my mom. She wanted me to see what my father was doing. We walked right in the front gates, tabloid photographers in tow. The place was brutal then, but it was nothing compared to what I saw sitting on the hill, spying on the compound with Kader.

Without my mother's watchful eye, four prisoners were dragged out for beating then shoved back in. Guards kicked and spat on an old man who'd fallen. A cart of bodies was wheeled out and disappeared. I wasn't quite sure I wanted to know where or for what purpose.

But worst of all were the little bodies amongst the prisoners.

"Why are there children down here?" I asked Kader.

"It's a quiet program one of your father's ministers instigated," Kader said, binoculars poised on his eyes. "Mixed children who get in trouble are sent here."

"Mixed children?"

"Raven and Kylaen parents," Kader said. To my perplexed look, he added, "It happens a lot more often in the slums of Norose. There are more Ravens here than you'd think."

"Define get in trouble."

"Stealing, shoplifting," Kader said.

"Are all kids from the slums sent here when they're caught? Not to a regular jail or a rehabilitation or even a school?"

Kader didn't respond. If I'd thought I couldn't hate my father any more...

"The next shift change is in half an hour," Kader said, looking at his watch. "I will go down there and get uniforms and bring them back. It's a good thing they mandate the use of masks."

"For guards," I noted bitterly.

"Yes, for guards," Kader said. "Because otherwise, they'd recognize their prince, who most of them still consider deceased." He was so calm, as if this were just another day in the office.

"Kader...what did you do before you were my guard?" I asked, realizing I'd never bothered to learn anything about him. No wonder he hated me so much.

He paused in mid-step. "Special Operations. But my wife got tired of wondering if I was going to come back alive. So I took a...cushy job." I noticed the gold band on his finger, and made a promise to myself to ask if I could meet his wife and personally thank her for letting me borrow her husband. I felt like that's something Theo would've done.

That's what Theo will do, I corrected myself.

"Stay here," Kader said, ending our conversation.

THEO

My only knowledge of time's passage was the sun beginning to set in the distance, reflecting orange streaks through the dirty windows high above us. The shift had changed three times during my time shoveling. That knowledge, I supposed, might've helped me had there not been three inches of iron around my legs.

Only pure stubbornness had kept me standing. I couldn't feel anything in my body—not my stomach, not my arms, not even my broken leg. My movement was dazed, and I wondered if they ever let the prisoners stop working to sleep.

To keep myself afloat, I forced myself to think of Galian. But I could only picture his eyes. I'd already forgotten what he looked like...

The presence was behind me again, the one that had been haunting me all day. Lightness entered my limbs when the shackles fell from my wrists. I swayed for a moment, blinking in exhaustion. Was someone letting me go?

But a cold, slimy hand encircled my wrist and pulled me away from the line.

"W-what are you doing?" My voice was scratchy, my throat parched from dehydration.

We stopped in front of another guard. I barely heard the conversation between them, but the look on the other guard's face snapped me to attention.

"I'll have her back before next shift."

I felt eyes on me, the same kind that had leered at my naked body in the hospital. And I knew I had to get away.

"Let *go* of me," I whimpered, my fight taken by exhaustion and the toxic fumes.

Helplessly, I searched for help amongst the rest of the guards. But their appreciative nods only made me more desperate to release the iron grip around my wrist.

"No, please." I clawed at his strong hand.

He didn't even look at me, just kept dragging me. I stuck my legs in the ground, only for them to give way with more than a tug. Bile rose in my throat and I shook as he tossed me into the office.

The door closed behind me, and I refused to get up. I wasn't going to *help* this—

We weren't alone. There was another man in the room, his face obscured by one of the face masks.

But his eyes looked just like my Galian's.

He would've wanted me to fight. And so, even if it killed me, I would fight these bastards.

I scooted back against the desk as one of the guards approached me. When he reached a hand out for me, I flung it away, kicking and scratching and fighting as hard as I could.

"Theo, stop!"

I screamed and closed my eyes, thrashing more wildly. Now my mind was starting to play tricks on me. I could've sworn I'd heard his voice underneath that mask, but that was impossible—

"Theo, stop, it's me!"

He ripped his mask off and I was now sure the noxious fumes had taken their effect on me—until I felt the gentle touch on my cheek.

"It's okay," he said, cupping my face gently. "I'm here."

"*A-amichai,*" I choked out, before tears of relief splashed down my face.

"I'm so sorry," he whispered into my hair. "Theo, I'm so..."

The man who I'd thought to be a guard addressed Galian. "Sire, we need to move."

"Right," Galian cupped my face. "We're going to sneak you out of here, get you on a plane, and—"

"What about them?" I asked, looking out at the rest of the prisoner camp.

"Them?" Galian followed my gaze. "*Them*? Theo, we can't—"

"So why do I get to live and they don't?" I asked, stepping back from him.

I remembered the children, the tumors, the man who stumbled into his own execution. The prisoners who arrived there every day, every *hour*. I'd been there for less than a day, but I loved these prisoners more than my own lieutenants. Raven, Kylaen, they were now my countrymen.

"*Why do I get to live and they don't?*" I repeated, needing an answer from Galian and knowing he'd never have one to satisfy me.

His shoulders slumped and the defeat in his eyes was evident. "Because I promised you on that island I wasn't going to let you die."

I shook my head. "Why is my life worth more than theirs? What makes me so important?"

"Because I love you."

"That's not good enough, Galian," I said, taking his hands in mine. "You told me on the island that you were too afraid of doing the right thing. You said you didn't have a choice. You didn't think you could make a difference."

"Theo—"

"But you made the choice to come here to save my life," I

pleaded, my eyes growing wet with tears. "You chose me over yourself, and now...*amichai*, now you can make a real difference. You just have to believe you can. You just have to do the right thing. Please, Galian." I swallowed hard. "Please don't leave them here."

GALIAN

The easy thing to do would've been to throw her over my shoulder and run like hell. An option that sounded tempting and a lot less dangerous. Before the island, I might've chosen that easy option. I would've been content to do the minimum and say I'd done my best and go to sleep at night believing that I'd tried.

But that wasn't going to fly with Theo. She expected the best of me, and I wanted to be the best for her. I wanted to prove to us both that I could be better.

Step one was *being* better. And for that, I was at a loss.

I glanced at Kader. "What can we do?"

He grunted and pulled off his mask. He rubbed a hand over his face and pinched the bridge of his nose.

"Kader—"

"Quiet." He looked out the window and tapped his hand against his face. "We might be able to convince them that we're transporting prisoners. I see mostly people arriving, but perhaps we could convince them that five need to leave."

"Five?" Theo said. "There's hundreds out there!"

"Theo, once we get out of here, I promise you, I *swear* to you, I will do everything in my power to shut this place down," I said, for lack of anything else to say. I glanced at Kader and then back to Theo. "But right now, five is all we can handle."

After a long pause, she sighed. "The youngest five you can get your hands on."

Kader tilted his head in agreement and handed her one of the spare uniforms we'd found. She dressed quickly, pulling the Kylaen uniform over the prison uniform. Balling up her long hair, she stuck it under the hat. I helped her pull some of it down to look like her hair was cropped short.

"And here." Kader handed her a gas mask. "Just keep your eyes down, and hold onto the gun."

I replaced my own gas mask, and suddenly the air was sweeter and my head clearer.

"What now, Kader?" I asked, my voice muffled by the mask.

Kader's voice was similarly garbled. "Gather the ones you want to save—*five*, Raven, do you understand? Any more, and you could jeopardize us all."

Her eyes flashed behind her mask, but she said nothing.

In support, I entwined my fingers through hers and squeezed.

"We have less than ten minutes to complete this mission. Are you sure this is what you want to do?" Kader asked.

"Yes," she said, with such force that I thought she might salute him.

Kader opened the door out into the processing plant main room and Theo dropped my hand. My heart pounded as I followed Kader's tall form and I kept my eyes glued to the ground.

Kader motioned behind his back to us and we separated from him, walking toward the line of Ravens hunched over the tall mound of raw material. We came closer, and I saw the bony arms, the sallow skin, and the faces of people I was effectively sentencing to die.

Theo must have made peace with it better than I, because she walked over to the two smallest and barked an order for the guards to unlock them. Kader was conferring with the head guards, and they nodded their approval.

Damn, I thought. *Kader's a little too good at this.*

Theo grabbed the shoulders of the two children, who began to openly weep in terror. It took everything in me not to step in and comfort them, but I was supposed to be an unfeeling guard. How these men and women could work there day in and day out without feeling was beyond me.

How my *father* could sanction this kind of behavior was beyond me. And I was determined to stop it once we got out of here. That thought alone was enough to pry me from the line of workers and follow Theo to the next group.

I noticed another guard staring at us, so I walked over to a prisoner and poked her with the edge of my gun.

"Um... work faster."

The woman cowered at the touch and fell to her knees. I could see bruising on her face and arms, and angrily added to the list of people I was going to murder.

She gazed up at me with wide, wondrous eyes.

"Angel!" The woman grabbed my arm. "It's Prince Galian, come back from the dead!"

My blood ran cold as the murmur rose through the ranks of the prisoners around her. I tried to free my arm, but she held on tight, screaming about how I'd returned as an angel from God to save them. Theo worked to free the woman's grip, glancing in panic back at the other guards.

"*Oi! What are you doing?*" The guards approached us and narrowed their eyes at me, as if seeing what the woman had.

"You ain't—"

Theo was quicker than I was, and slammed her gun into his gut. Our cover was most assuredly blown, so I grabbed her arm and dragged her away from the line.

"Galian, we can't leave them," Theo cried, clawing at the prisoners starting to gather and scream in the chaos. I heard gunshots and broke into a run, bursting out of the back doors and spotting an idling prisoner transport.

"*Stop! Stop them!*"

More gunshots cracked behind us, and the guards fell down. Kader appeared behind them, overtaking us and sprinting towards one of the prison transport trucks. He flew into the front seat and Theo and I clamored into the back. We'd barely gotten inside before Kader set the truck into motion.

Bullet holes appeared in the metal near Theo's head and I yanked her down to the ground, covering her body with mine until they'd stopped.

THEO

We rode for hours in silence, me staring at the floor of the transport truck and Galian staring at me. Galian's guard, Kader, was at the wheel, and from all the turns and stops and starts, he was doing a good job of losing anyone who might've followed us. The back of the transport truck remained open, the door slamming against the jam at every turn. But the longer we drove, the more the landscape changed—from rocky, mountainous plains to greener pastures.

Guilt ate at me, and I couldn't even bring myself to cry. I didn't deserve to cry or seek comfort in my *amichai's* arms as much as I wanted to. Not when I'd failed to save anyone but myself.

Kader stopped the van and for a moment, I clenched my hand around Galian's, afraid that I had been betrayed again. But when I stepped out of the vehicle, a slick, black car was parked in an abandoned parking lot. Galian tugged at my hand and gently helped me out of the transport truck, allowing me to lean on him as we sat on the plush leather seats.

The luxury was a sharp contrast to the world I'd just left. I hadn't been able to sleep or eat all day, and Kylaens rode around in plush cars.

"Theo." Galian's voice was soft and comforting. "Are you okay?"

I could still see the children I'd left behind. I couldn't bring myself to imagine what those cruel guards would do to them. I just hoped if they were to die, it would be quick.

I didn't even realize I was crying until Galian's hand brushed away a tear. The movement was soft and full of love, and it destroyed me. I collapsed into a sobbing heap, spasms of guilt and relief taking turns in my heart. My *amichai* held me, whispering sweet nothings of comfort. It was a long time before his guard returned to the car, presumably to give me the privacy to fall apart. I would be forever grateful for that.

But return he did, and we left the empty parking lot for a

destination unknown and, yet...I knew where they were taking me. Galian's naive optimism was one thing, but my other savior was a touch more realistic.

When the door opened again, I saw what I'd been both dreading and hoping for. A plane—Kylaen, but a plane nonetheless. I was going home.

And I was also leaving my *amichai*.

"We could go back." His voice was strained as he wrapped me in his arms.

"I would never ask that of you."

"If it meant I could be with you, I'd do it."

I leaned into him, resting my head against his chin.

"I love you," he whispered.

"And that's why I have to go," I said, twisting in his arms to look at him.

I remembered the cave, his fingers wrapped around mine, the closeness of our bodies. I remembered when *amichai* had rolled off my tongue, when he'd asked me to come back with him. But that was the island, where things were easy and simple, and there wasn't a war and his father and all the millions of things standing between us.

I loved him for his naive optimism, but that naivety had almost gotten me killed. Even worse, it might've signed the death warrant of all of the prisoners in Mael that day.

"We can't... This isn't..." I closed my eyes as two more tears fell. "There's no way us being together could ever be a reality."

His eyes burned with fury and anguish, and it broke my heart. "I am *not* giving up on you Theophilia Kallistrate. I promised you I wasn't going to let you die, and now I'm promising you that this *isn't over*." The hand on my cheek clenched, and he sucked in a breath. "You

245 | S. USHER EVANS

and me, we wouldn't have made it this far just to be separated. God doesn't have such a sick sense of humor, remember?"

I swallowed, my own words sounding harsh in his mouth.

"Look at me." He gently lifted my chin.

"I love you," I whispered.

And he kissed me, tasting sweeter than anything I'd had in my life. "Promise me you won't give up," he whispered.

"Galian—"

"Sire." Kader stood behind us, a stoic expression on his face. I envied him for having no feelings about our impending separation. "I have a temporary passcode to get her out of Kylaen airspace. But the guard on duty is only here for another hour and..."

"I'm not ready," Galian said, more to me than to him.

"Sire. She needs to go."

I pressed my lips to his once more, burning this memory into my mind and savoring every second. I would need this in the weeks and months to follow, when memories of Mael threatened to overtake my mind. I'd leaned on Galian to get me through it the first time, and I would need every tool in my arsenal to make it past the aftereffects.

Without another word, I ripped myself from him and took the passcode from Kader. I marched toward the plane, glad that Galian couldn't see the emotion in my eyes, grateful that I couldn't see his because it would test my resolve to leave.

I climbed into the plane and settled in, the familiar feeling of a joystick between my legs and the hum of a jet engine reminding me of the person I used to be. The soldier, the captain, the...

My gaze drifted up to the figure standing on the runway.

Without another thought, I released the brakes and screamed into flight.

TWENTY

GALIAN

It was as if I'd never left.

I sat next to my mother and across from my brother at an exquisite table made of the finest dark wood, expertly carved with the Kylaen symbol. Seated at the head of the table was my father, resplendent in his uniform, even deigning to wear his fancy crown while he ate his meal. I knew it was a warning to me, but I found myself unable to care. After facing my own mortality more times than I could even count, I was suddenly unafraid of what he could do to me. Or perhaps it was the memory of Theo, reminding me that, unlike most people in our countries, I actually had a choice.

Our fine dinnerware clinked as we daintily nibbled at the courses of food placed in front of us. I was full after the first appetizer. But for my mother, I pretended to eat the soup, the salad, the main course of duck and potatoes, and the light dessert of ice cream in the absence of a conversation topic.

I counted my mother's gaze flickering toward my father at least three times per minute, whereas my brother, the heir to the very seat the man sat in, kept his eyes glued to his plate. The entire spectacle had been eye roll-worthy before the island, but now it was downright laughable. Everyone lived in fear of Grieg, but he was just a man. I truly had nothing to fear—unlike those children I'd left behind.

I swallowed hard, becoming even less hungry than I was before. I'd been so intent on saving them, I'd promised Theo I would do my best. Yet there I sat in front of the man who could stop everything, and my tongue was glued to the roof of my mouth.

I looked down at my melting ice cream and forced myself to take another small bite, but my stomach protested as soon as the cold, sweet mixture hit my stomach.

"Something wrong, Gally?" My mother's voice cut through the silence of the table.

"Just not used to this much food," I responded lightly.

Both she and Rhys had pressed me for details about my time on the island, but I couldn't bring myself to talk about it. It hurt too much, especially since there was an empty seat to my left where Theo should've been sitting.

Although I was sure that given the opportunity, Theo would have rather spent a year on the island than share a meal with my father. I imagined the fireworks that would ensue if that ever happened and smiled to myself.

"So I hear that there was a prisoner escape at Mael," my father said across the dinner table. He'd obviously noticed my happiness and wanted to destroy it. "Your Raven woman fled across the ocean."

I grunted in acknowledgment.

"Boy, when the king of Kylae addresses you, you answer *yes, sire*," he snapped at me. I hadn't said "yes, sire" in my entire life, and I sure as hell wasn't about to start now.

"Grieg, don't harass the boy," my mother said.

Even though it was a private family dinner, it was still dangerous for her to correct him at all. On his left side, Rhys tossed me a nervous look, as if he, too, was waiting for the explosion.

Instead, my father turned back to his meal. "So, boy, when do you think you'll return to active duty?"

"Grieg, he *just* got back," my mother gasped, giving him a look that told him exactly what she thought about my military service. "Give him a month, at least!"

"Korina, his fellow soldiers don't get to relax at home with their mommies," my father snarled at her, and making my blood boil. "He's a man, and he needs—"

"I don't think I'm going back," I said, the confidence in my voice surprising everyone in the room, myself included.

"What was that, boy?" My father looked nearly apoplectic and I wasn't sure that I'd help him if he collapsed with a heart attack.

"I said," I smiled, loving this feeling of control, "I'm resigning my commission and returning to the hospital."

My father's face turned a bright red as his rage boiled. "And what makes you think I'll let you do that?"

"Because I don't give a flying fuck what you think anymore," I said, enjoying the shock that rippled across the table. "I'm done fighting your little war—"

"That Raven whore put some ideas in your head, huh?" My father looked as if he were about to explode, and I rather hoped he would. "She sucked your dick and suddenly you're a pacifist!"

"I didn't need her to tell me what a bastard you are," I said, leaning back in my chair. "Oh, Mael's perfectly safe. Isn't that what you said? Guess what I found on that island? Your grandfather's secret testing lab. Very illuminating how they used to test barethium on *humans*. I saw the photos."

My mother's spoon clattered to the ground as she stared at my father. "What?"

He swallowed, but didn't refute my claim.

"And besides that, when's the last time the Ravens actually attacked *us*? When's the last time you actually considered the possibility of peace with them? When was the last time you did anything to try to decouple our economy from the business of killing people? Or is that *too difficult* for you?"

"You better watch yourself, boy," My father growled. "I can send you to Mael and—"

"Go ahead," I dared, standing up. "I'll be sure to hold a press conference from there about how you *left* me on the island for two months."

The room fell silent and my father didn't refute it. I could see the horror on my mother's face and the uncertainty on my brother's. But I didn't dare move my eyes away from my father's.

"You had the entirety of the Kylaen air forces at your disposal, and *Kader* is the one who found me." Blood pounded faster in my ears with every moment Grieg didn't refute me. "It was better for you to just wait for me to die of my own accord. Three days you waited before the mourning propaganda started. You had *no* intention of coming to get me."

"Gally." My mother was sobbing.

"Tell me I'm wrong, *Father*," I growled, pointing at the man. "Tell me you put your forces towards my retrieval. Tell me you were more worried about whether your youngest son lived or died. Tell me that, I'll suit back up and fight your stupid war."

My father sat back, the look on his face telling enough. He was cut from the same cloth as his father, and his father's father. The kind of man who knew—and didn't care—that building processing plants for barethium would result in the death of anyone with long-term exposure to it. He was the kind of man who would sentence children to death for simply existing.

Even more galling: he was the kind of man who would maintain the status quo because it was too hard to try to change anything. And that, more than anything else, was why I decided then and there that I no longer wished to be his son.

I turned to leave, and my father's voice floated over to me as I flung open the door. "Did you help that woman escape?"

"*Yes, sire,*" I said with a flourished bow before storming out of the family room, feeling freer than I'd ever felt in my life.

And as I thought about how much I wanted to tell Theo, to hear her once again tell me how proud she was of me, the ache in my heart returned.

THEO

The hospitals in Rave were much filthier than the ones in Kylae, but I was eternally grateful. I was home, I was in my country, with my people—as screwed up and helpless as they were.

This was where I belonged.

So why couldn't I stop missing him?

"You're damned lucky, is what you are," Lanis repeated, sitting in the chair to my right. My old chief mechanic hadn't left my side since I landed the Kylaen plane in the airstrip of my forward operating base. He was right; I *was* damned lucky that no one had shot me out of the sky. But my pilot code had given them enough pause to call Lanis to the tower, and he'd recognized my voice.

There was an audible gasp when they saw the guard uniform. Everyone in Rave knew what the Mael uniforms looked like.

Lanis dragged me to the nearest hospital, and the doctors did as much as they could for me. The nurses provided me with a clean hospital gown and propped my leg up on a pillow. They gave me a small ration of food, though it was more than I'd ever eaten on the island. No one pressed me for details on what had happened to me, and I let them assume the worst.

I wasn't sure if I wanted to tell them about the island. About Galian. It was partially because I didn't want them to know I'd been so close to the prince and *hadn't* killed him, but more so because I didn't want to admit what had really happened out loud.

No matter how long I'd stood in the shower and scrubbed at my skin, the stench of Mael clung to me and my sleep had been plagued by nightmares of tumored children shoveling black stones.

My heart was at war with itself now. For as much as I loved Galian, I hated his country. I hated what they were doing in the name of their own war machine. I hated the callousness with which they treated their enemies and their own citizens. That Galian had come from such a place was a testament to how good a person he really was.

As much as I struggled, as much as I told myself it was a futile effort, my heart still resided with him. That island had bonded us, and I knew in the bottom of my soul that I would never be truly happy again until the war was over, the prisoners were free, and I was in his arms.

But that thought only made my heart hurt again. Without Galian there to fill it up, my optimism was woefully depleted.

I remembered his promise to me. He'd said it wasn't over. But Kylae and Rave had been at war for fifty years; what could he do?

I heard a commotion outside my room, and Lanis went to check it for me. Before he got two steps, the door swung open.

A man I'd only seen on the news walked into my room and it was as surreal as the day I'd first laid eyes on Galian. President Bayard was shorter than he appeared in photos, but his hair was oilier and slicked back. His black goatee shimmered on his dark skin—darker, I noticed, through the use of caked-on makeup.

As if that weren't enough to surprise me, twenty reporters and five cameras shoved into my cramped hospital room after him, chattering and grunting like a horde. Their lenses focused on Bayard and an aide handed him a microphone.

I tossed a confused look at Lanis, who looked astonished as I was, and I nervously flattened my hospital gown. The president was positively beaming as he adjusted himself in front of the camera, taking almost no notice of me. Up close, I could see the makeup falling into his creased face, and he looked much older than he seemed in photos.

"Ready?" He nodded to the first cameraman, who gave him a countdown. Then he began with a booming, "Good evening, fellow citizens of Raven. I bring you incredible tidings of joy on this beautiful and most glorious day—another in our beautiful independence."

The familiarity of his voice and his words were at once calming and unnerving. I'd heard him on the radio since I was a little girl—he'd been my president for most of my life—but to have him there in that room...

"Today, I'm here in the hospital room of one of the many brave pilots in our Raven fleet, Captain Theo Kallistrate." He paused to gesture to me in the bed, and I wondered if I should wave or something. My hands were sweaty with nerves. "The good captain has endured great trials since she was considered lost at sea two months ago. We had already placed a star on the wall in her honor."

There was no such wall, although the politicians talked about it all the time. If there were truly a wall where all fallen Ravens were honored, it would contain more stars than the night sky.

Bayard continued. "But this morning, she arrived..." He paused for dramatic effect. "...in a prisoner uniform from Mael."

A gasp arose from the reporters, and I wondered if they'd been paid to do that.

"You see, our good captain was held prisoner by the Kylaens, forced to work in the mines in unspeakable terror. For a whole two months, you see...and she *survived*."

I clenched my jaw; so that was what they were doing with me. I was now to be the latest of Rave's Celebrated Heroes. Perhaps I'd get an increase in my food rations.

"Captain Kallistrate returned to us with not just herself, but ten of our Raven brothers and sisters in the ship she stole from the Kylaens."

My heart fell to my stomach. I hadn't rescued anyone. It was one thing to make up my trials at Mael, but I was not going to be made a hero. Not when I could still the faces of the children I hadn't saved. I remembered the little boy with a tumor in his stomach. The woman—it was too much to lie about.

"President—"

With a great wave of his hand, he took mine in his and kissed them. His lips were thick and slimy against my skin.

"You have my humblest thanks for bringing our Raven brothers and sisters home," he said, loud enough for the cameras to catch it, but with a look that only I saw.

I swallowed my confession. It was clear I had no say in what was going on.

He turned to address the rest of the room and the cameras again. "Captain, or, dare I say, *Major* Kallistrate." He smiled at me. I supposed that was my promotion announcement. "From this point on, you shall be an orphan no more," he said to the cameras. "For Rave is your mother, Rave is your father, Rave is your brother, and your sister. And you, my dear Theo, are our *'neechai*."

A few of the nurses broke out into loud tears, overcome with emotions. Bayard smiled for the cameras, holding my hand and letting the photographers take a few photos.

"That's a wrap, sir," the cameraman said, taking the camera off his shoulder.

"Excellent," Bayard said, releasing my hand and his smarmy expression. "You'll do well, Theo. Very well."

"What is this about?"

Bayard adjusted the cuffs on his expensive jacket; it seemed out of place in a country so desperate for cash. "We're weary of war, weary of hardships, and some think it would be best if our country returned to the sovereign rule of Kylae. Back to being the king's slaves."

The thought made me sick to my stomach, and I told him as much.

"The country needs someone to believe in, someone who's been to the other side and *chose* to come home. Someone to stand in front of a camera and remind our mothers why they're sending their sons and daughters to war. Someone to rally the troops."

I cringed inwardly. Galian had said his father would do the same thing about his own death. After what I had been through, I wanted this war to be over. I didn't want to be a pawn any more. But I also knew an opportunity when I saw one.

"What do I get in return?"

He laughed. "They said you were smart, but cunning I did not expect," he said, sizing me up. "Well, my dear *kallistrate*, if you play nice in front of the cameras for a few months, I shall give you a place by my side in the President's cabinet."

My heart beat faster as he spoke of all the benefits of being his right-hand woman. But all I could think about was that I'd be in the thick of the Raven leadership. Perhaps in a position of power, I could find a way to stop the war.

Perhaps I could find a way back to my *amichai*.

"Well, Theo," Bayard said, interrupting my thoughts. "Will you answer the call?"

The flame of hope reignited in my soul.

THEO AND GALIAN'S ADVENTURE
CONTINUES IN BOOK 2

THE
CHASM
THE MADION WAR TRILOGY

AVAILABLE NOW

WWW.SGR-PUB.COM

ALSO BY S. USHER EVANS

DEMON SPRING TRILOGY

Three years ago, Jack Grenard's wife was brutally murdered by demons. Now, along with his partner Cam Macarro, he's trying to rebuild his life in Atlanta. But on a routine investigation, they find a demon who saves instead of kills. They must discover who she is before Demon Spring, the quadrennial breach between the human world and demon realm, when all hell—literally—breaks loose.

The Demon Spring Trilogy is the first urban fantasy from S. Usher Evans and will be released in 2018 in eBook, Paperback, and Hardcover.

The Razia Series

Lyssa Peate is living a double life as a planet discovering scientist and a space pirate bounty hunter. Unfortunately, neither life is going very well. She's the least wanted pirate in the universe and her brand new scientist intern is spying on her. Things get worse when her intern is mistaken for her hostage by the Universal Police.

The Razia Series is a four-book space opera series and is available now for eBook, Audiobook. Paperback, and Hardcover.

ALSO BY S. USHER EVANS

The Lexie Carrigan Chronicles

Lexie Carrigan thought she was weird enough until her family drops a bomb on her—she's magical. Now the girl who's never made waves is blowing up her nightstand and no one seems to want to help her. That is, until a kindle gentleman shows up with all the answers. But Lexie finds out being magical is the least weird thing about her.

Spells and Sorcery is the first book in the Lexie Carrigan Chronicles, and is available now in eBook, Paperback, Audiobook, and Hardcover.

empath

Lauren Dailey is in break-up hell, but if you ask her she's doing just great. She hears a mysterious voice promising an easy escape from her problems and finds herself in a brand new world where she has the power to feel what others are feeling. Just one problem—there's a dragon in the mountains that happens to eat Empaths. And it might be the source of the mysterious voice tempting her deeper into her own darkness.

Empath is a stand-alone fantasy that is available now in eBook, Paperback, and Hardcover.

ACKNOWLEDGEMENTS

Dani, thank you for teaching me the proper grammar for first-person, past tense. Anita, thank you for your patience and your artistry.

Special thanks go to the hordes of beta-readers who helped me pass the time between when the book was finished and publication. Jessa and Theo's Plane (OTP), Liz, Julia, Caitlin, Amanda, Megan, Fiona, Julie and so many others who checked it out on Wattpad. I'd like to think that every one of you has a stake in making this book the best that it can possibly be.

Speaking of stakes...the Kickstarter backers. Thanks to everyone who participated in the preorder campaign. Specifically, Theresa Snyder, Shanks, Elizabeth F., Robyn Bennis, Patricia Lynne, Mom, Evan B., Rachel Caine, Gracen, Kate The Majestic Narwhal, Amanda Perry, Cassie Shaunfield Gilmon, Emily from Emily Reads Everything, Natalie & Kevin, Nick N., Caleb Sledd, Liz Meldon (again), Anna M., Kari Ann Ramadorai, Anonymous, Erica, Brian G., Isabel Perez, Diana Pinguicha, Becca Stillo, My Biggest FanGirl Caitlyn McIntosh, Christina Termini, Michelle Bryan, Julia (again), Amanda Mayer, Christopher Severino, Sergei Lempert, Charles Anchors, Ellen Gray, David Kudler, Kayla Valderas, @julies_cr8tve, Pookie, Laura T., Lisa Henson, Mariam Khella, Meradeth, Cyra Schaefer, Hechunzi Sui, Holly Bryan, Taylor Winsor, Courtney Poucher, Michelle Falconer, Allen W. Shepherd, Kimberly L., Morgan Stillo, Megan, Eli Isenberg, and Kelly Sedinger, MC, and Sky. You guys are the most wonderful people.

ABOUT THE AUTHOR

S. Usher Evans was born and raised in Pensacola, Florida. After a decade of fighting bureaucratic battles as an IT consultant in Washington, DC, she suffered a massive quarter-life-crisis. She decided fighting dragons was more fun than writing policy, so she moved back to Pensacola to write books full-time. She currently resides with her two dogs, Zoe and Mr. Biscuit, and frequently can be found plotting on the beach.

Visit S. Usher Evans online at:
http://www.susherevans.com/

Twitter: www.twitter.com/susherevans
Facebook: www.facebook.com/susherevans
Instagram: www.instagram.com/susherevans

Made in the USA
Columbia, SC
20 August 2018